D1094140

# A BOOK
# DRAGON

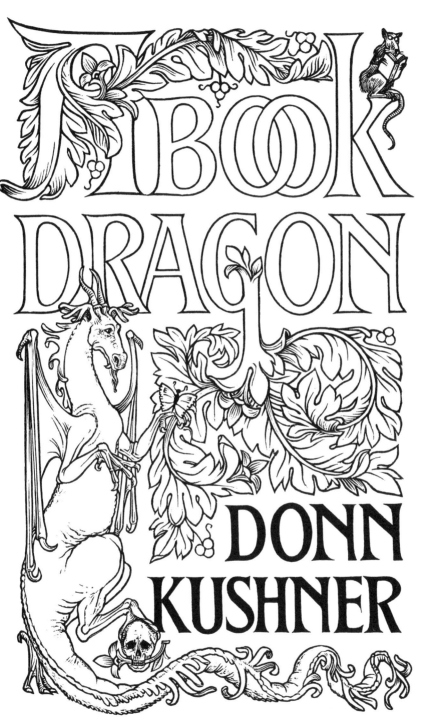

# BOOK DRAGON

# DONN KUSHNER

MACMILLAN OF CANADA
A Division of Canada Publishing Corporation

CANADIAN CATALOGUING IN PUBLICATION DATA
Kushner, Donn, date
  A book dragon
ISBN 0-7715-9515-8
I. Jackson, Nancy Ruth. II. Title.

PS8571.U83B66  1987     jC813'.54     C87-094136-4

Edited by Patricia Kennedy and Mary Cash

 Illustration and Design by
Nancy Ruth Jackson

Marginal note by Irish scribe on page ix cited in *Christmas Crackers* by J. J. Norwich, Allen Lane, 1980.

We gratefully acknowledge the support of the Ontario Arts Council in the publication of this book.

**Macmillan of Canada**
A Division of Canada Publishing Corporation
Toronto, Ontario, Canada

Printed in Canada

FOR EVA

He prayeth best, who loveth best
All things both great and small;
For the dear God who loveth us,
He made and loveth all.

S. T. Coleridge
*The Rime of the Ancient Mariner*

''Pleasant to me is the glittering of the sun upon
these margins, because it flickers so.''

# A DRAGON AND HIS GRANDMOTHER

WE SELDOM HEAR OF DRAGONS NOWADAYS. IT IS EASY to believe that they never existed at all. But many years ago people knew that there were dragons, just as they knew there were angels and devils, witches and gnomes, and, on occasion, banshees and leprechauns. Even if they saw no dragons in their own neighborhoods, they were sure that some could be found in far, unknown, fearful places. So that, in old maps of unexplored lands we can still see blank areas with the warning words, ''Here there bee dragons.''

The maps are all filled in now; the empty spaces bear names like Caracas, and Vladivostok, and Chicago. Dragons aren't mentioned at all. But there are dragons alive today, at least one of them. This is his story.

ONESUCH WAS — AND STILL IS, FOR THAT MATTER — THE last of a family of dragons that lived over five hundred years ago in a limestone hill, honeycombed with caverns, above the village of Serpent Grimsby near the south coast of England. The dark mouth of the family's cavern opened towards an ugly tangled scrub forest that ended, at the lap of the hill, in an evil bog: land which few men entered by choice and still fewer left. From the cavern, the dragons could see the tip of the village church spire over the crest of the next hill and, past this, the square towers and crenellated walls of the Earl's castle.

The castle had been built in the time of Nonesuch's great-grandfather. While lurking in the forest above the building site, he had become so interested in watching the walls of the donjon rise that when he came down for a snack of fat cattle, he found the circle almost completed. The drovers were able to herd the cattle inside and drop a crude gate, strong enough to keep out the dragon, who was of a peaceable disposition and too lazy to break it down. Later, he could only sniff sadly at the roasting meat as the guards and the workmen feasted on three of the cows. They had a fine time, with their ale barrels, and the smoke rising in the clear air, and their songs rising too, in praise of their own cleverness. When they were full, at the bidding of good Father John, the Earl's chaplain, they all knelt to thank the Lord for saving their animals from the evil dragon, whom they took to be the Devil himself.

Such setbacks often seemed to happen nowadays, None-such's grandmother told him. In the past, dragons, especially those of her own family, had been quicker, fiercer, subtler, more wily than they were now. The young dragon — he was not quite fifty years old at this time, of a clear luminous green, and his scales moved over each other with scarcely a squeak — listened to his grandmother with rapt attention, gazing at her with eager yellow eyes.

Nonesuch had never known his mother. Shortly after his birth, she was seized with a great longing for solitude and dryness and flew south, to brood over the sands of the Sahara Desert. Sometimes her vast form could be seen by the fearful Egyptians, sprawled atop the Pyramid of Cheops. She crouched before the Sphinx, both motionless for days, until the stone monster's patience had, at last, won. Then Nonesuch's mother had flown off towards the sources of the Nile. Who knew where she was now?

Whatever she herself had done in the past, the grandmother now stayed indoors. Nonesuch never tired of hearing her recount his family's history. He would sprawl on the flat floor of the cavern, by the entrance, sometimes raising a wing to keep the least ray of sunlight from his grandmother's eyes, while she lay as far from daylight as possible, by her pile of treasure.

His grandmother told Nonesuch of the legendary founder of their race, the great Gorm, who, it was said, lumbered up from the black swamps when men still lived in caves. Gorm used to lie down among these cave-dwellers and let them pound him with clubs and try their flinty spears on his tough hide, much as a dog enjoys his master's scratches. Then, when they were worn out with their useless efforts, Gorm would lazily select a few of his attackers for lunch.

She told of cunning Hrafnagel, who would crouch in the brown grass of Salisbury Plain within sight of the pillars of Stonehenge on summer evenings, picking off the blue-painted Druids as they whirled in ecstasy among the shadows.

Her memory ranged then to the Continental branch of the family: to the mighty Feuerschlange, who ruled in the dark forests of northern Germany. With his tail alone, this fearsome beast once swept a whole phalanx of steel-clad soldiers into a small lake. Then he set the lake boiling with his fiery breath and ate his dinner cooked, picking each soldier out of his steel shell. Nonesuch's father had seen people do much the same thing with snails, the grandmother added for the sake of information, though she disapproved of her son's interest in human eating habits. ("What good can come of it?" she would remark.)

And then her mind, which sometimes could not remember events of the same day, took a great leap backwards. In the beginning, his grandmother told Nonesuch, dragons had chosen to separate themselves from the dinosaurs, to whom they were distantly related, except for being so much more intelligent.

She described that terrible time, millions and millions of years ago, when a huge stone from the sky struck the earth and filled the heavens with dust, so that the vegetation which fed dinosaurs and their prey died, and in time the immense beasts died too. She told, almost as if she were seeing it now, how the ancestors of the dragons flew high above the dust clouds, resting only on the mountain tops, feeding on the ancestors of sure-footed mountain goats and other such frugal, hardy creatures. Below them, in the thick murk, the dragons could hear the plaintive groans of dinosaurs, who seemed more ready to die than to admit how their world had changed and seek new food in new places. Occasionally a pterodactyl, a great winged reptile, would swoop up into the sunlight, then, confused by so much clarity, descend again into the dying forests. ''They were so stupid,'' the grandmother said, wagging her head with a sour, disapproving tone, as if she were speaking of creatures alive now, not those dead for millions of years. ''No true dragon could ever tolerate stupidity.''

''But Grandmother,'' Nonesuch said respectfully, for he knew she didn't like to be contradicted, ''some of our ancestors have done foolish things. You've said so yourself.'' He remembered her past stories. ''Most of the time,'' he added.

His grandmother reared back her head and almost rose up on her legs; her dim eyes glowed fiercely. ''Foolish? Yes! Improvident? More often than not! Never counting the cost! At times, frankly, insane! But not stupid! Any true dragon could always tally up the costs of its actions, could always foretell that it was heading for disaster, if it chose. But there are more important choices!''

Then, her eyes sending out pulses of dull light, as pride and sorrow swelled within her, his grandmother told of the valiant, unfortunate Schatzwache, who, from high above the Caucasus mountains, spotted a vein of pure gold exposed by a sudden geological fault. Obedient to the great law of all dragons, ''Guard your treasure,'' Schatzwache settled down on the shining surface, covering it with his wide wings and long tail, hardly leaving it even to search for food. Finally, when he was so weak that he could no longer fly, he was set upon by scores of knights with two-handed swords and hundreds of bushy-bearded peasants with long axes. He gave a good account of himself before his enemies hacked him to pieces, and his green blood mingled with theirs. But the dragon's blood burned down into the gold itself, giving it a magnificent blue-green sheen: the ''dragon-gold'' from which the crowns of all the Czars of Russia were fashioned.

"Yes, guard your treasure," the grandmother repeated. "A dragon without a treasure is nothing but an ugly flying reptile, with even less dignity than a salamander!" Then, her nostrils pinched together, she added, "With less dignity than a turtle, and with no more than a toad."

Nonesuch's grandmother had many sayings like this, which she brought out at more or less appropriate times. "Never kill anything you won't eat," she would say, adding in a milder tone, "Why waste the energy?" Or, "Be dauntless, valiant, tragic, whatever you like; but don't be stupid." Or, "If you must fight, find a worthy foe." (Often adding with a shake of her head, "If you're lucky enough to come across one these days.") But usually, even if she had said it before, she would end her list of precepts with: "Always guard your treasure!"

So, dreaming, remembering her family's past glory, her cracked, scaly head nodding, her great eyes closing and winking, the grandmother drooled and mumbled over her own pile of treasure: over the gilded sword hilts, the blackened silver arm rings with crudely cut sapphires, the gold coins in rotten wooden chests, the skulls and neck-bones encircled with diadems and jewelled chains.

At the very back of the heap, against the cavern wall, were layers of stacked shields, elbow-deep in tarnished silver coins, all resting on a massive carved door that seemed to have been torn by its hinges from some castle hall. Sometimes she dragged herself up on the pile of treasure and thrust the door aside with her claws. Behind it was a narrow tunnel that slanted steeply downwards. The grandmother would stick her head into the tunnel and withdraw it again. Rarely she entered as far as her shoulders; only once with all her body but the tip of her tail. She let no one else enter.

When she had looked long enough down the tunnel, she withdrew her head, moodily thrust the door back in place, weighed it down with the shields and coins, and spread herself out so that a claw and a wing, at least, covered part of the pile of treasure; then she would resume her thoughts, and her slumbers, and her tales of the old days.

Almost always, when she had given her account of her family's history and a catalogue of the rules by which they lived, the grandmother would heave a sigh that made the cavern's walls shudder, and remark that their race had declined.

For several generations now, they had lost the ability to breathe fire. The only traces that remained of this once mighty power were the internal fires that caused their eyes to glow and to give forth enough light for the dragons to find their way in pitch darkness. And, she added, that kept their blood warm, so that they were active in all weathers, not sluggish in fall and sleeping in winter like the lowly reptiles that sometimes dared to claim kinship with them.

More important, dragons seemed to have missed their path in dealing with humans. The grandmother's words were saddest when she spoke of these creatures. She had watched them closely and felt that no good could come of them. They were small, soft, fearful, but resourceful: capable of infinite guile. Sometimes, she suspected, they regarded dragons only as problems, not as catastrophes. She confessed to a terrible foreboding that human cunning would finally triumph over the dragons' strength and sinewy grace, over their fierce courage and joy of combat.

And after a silence that might last half an hour, the grandmother would declare that it was not through fear that most dragons now refrained from eating human flesh, but through suspicion. When they spoke of their reluctance to eat people, dragons usually mentioned how difficult it was to separate them from their clothes: the thick leather jerkins; the layer upon layer of petticoats that bunched up so in your stomach; then, the armor, the shin-guards, the chain mail, and all the rest!

But these weren't the real reasons, the grandmother said, winking wisely. She had finally decided that dragons did not eat human flesh because they mistrusted it.

They were wise to do so. She herself had flown over battlefields and seen thousands of human bodies, drying in the wind, infecting all the air with their stench. Despite this, she had hovered over the field for hours to watch and learn.

She had concluded that since humans killed, but did not eat, each other there must be something terribly wrong with their flesh. "And your cousin will learn what it is one day," she said. "You'll see if he doesn't!"

She was referring to Nonesuch's mean cousin, Cauchemar, a mud-colored beast who was usually seen out of the corner of one's eye, slithering away, and who was now the only one of the family who ate humans.

But even though he was the terror of Serpent Grimsby and its surroundings, Cauchemar probably did humans more good than harm. He ate mainly murderers and other violent criminals, his appetite excited by the scent of evil and terror that rose from their flesh. After such a meal, Cauchemar would lie for hours at the mouth of his own cavern with an expression on his face that showed he had acquired as much knowledge as nourishment from his victim.

He was also fond of liquor. Sometimes he would eat a drunkard who had fallen asleep after going out behind the village inn to count the stars. But even a very little alcohol affected Cauchemar powerfully. He would then lie on the ground for hours, staring up at the stars himself, his great eyes like moons come down to earth, crooning uncouth songs.

"Watch out for Cauchemar," the grandmother often told Nonesuch, nodding mysteriously. The remark made no sense at all. Nonesuch, who had not yet reached his full growth, measured a good thirty feet from nose to tail, and his wingspan was still greater. Cauchemar, who was smaller, had stopped growing ten years ago. Nonesuch ranged high in the air for the joy of flying; sometimes he would overthrow young pines with his claws as he passed, just to see them fall. He considered himself a match for almost anyone, especially his cousin. But his grandmother continued to warn him, looking at him as if there were yet more behind her words.

And sometimes her words were more puzzling still. She would mutter herself to sleep with "Turtles and toads; turtles and toads", in tones of such distaste that it seemed there could be no forms of life lower than these.

# CHAPTER II

# TURTLES, TOADS, AND BUTTERFLIES

# N

ONESUCH ALWAYS BECAME
UNCOMFORTABLE WHEN
his grandmother spoke so slightingly of
turtles and toads, though he certainly did
not contradict her. Her words reminded him
of an unimportant event in his childhood,
one that he had never thought it worth while
to mention to anyone. Whenever he remembered this incident, he told himself that it
was foolish even to think about it, let alone
bring it into his elders' important conversation.

He had just turned ten and was rejoicing
in his ability to fly, to travel great distances,
to look down on all the petty earth-bound
creatures. One day, soaring above a wide
beech forest, he saw a wink of blue far
below. Circling, he realized it was a small,
perfectly round pool shaded among the
smooth boles of the beech trees. Nonesuch
was still childish enough to be curious at a
new, pretty thing, though he was trying to
overcome this. He glided down into the
forest. This took skill as well as courage,
since his wingspan was already greater
than the distance between many of the trees.
He had to twist and bank to avoid the trunks
and slip between the branches. As he de-

scended he thought, with some pride, that all the full-grown dragons were too large to follow him and, with a feeling he could not identify, that soon he would also be too large.

Nonesuch landed by the pool's brim. When the surface became still again after the wind of his flight, he looked over at his own face, framed in the reflection of beech trunks. His features were still childlike, without the fierce, proud angles of a proper adult dragon. The water was smooth, the day hot and dusty. He thrust his head in, almost up to the eyes. Then he looked up at the beech trees, down at their crooked reflection in the rippling water, and let his eyes sweep the surface of the pond to enjoy the double image of a bright-yellow butterfly with a blue star on each wing.

"Well," a grumpy voice remarked, "I hope you'll leave some water for the rest of us!"

Nonesuch opened his eyes wide. Directly before him a head rose out of the water, a horny, disapproving head on a long, wrinkled neck that emerged from a hard greenish-orange shell.

The dragon took his head completely out of the water. In the wave this created the turtle's head disappeared for a moment, then poked up again by a lily-pad. To show that he had not descended to the pool for frivolous reasons, Nonesuch took a deep drink of water and announced stiffly, "I was thirsty."

"I can well believe it, with all those fires inside you," the turtle replied. "We were watching you," he added. "It's very rare to see one of your lot so close. Usually you stay above the tree-tops, which is quite close enough."

Nonesuch decided not to take offence at the remarks of such a lowly creature. "Our wings are too vast and broad; their sweep is too mighty for the confined air of the forests," he replied loftily. This was how they talked back in the cavern.

"Yes," hissed a thin, very high voice, which Nonesuch still heard — for dragons had sharp ears: they could hear a sheep bleat or a maiden scream three valleys away. The butterfly was speaking. Now it continued: "I've seen them bouncing from the tree trunks like hailstones. They have no control at all!" Then, as if to show what control was, the butterfly traced an intricate, beautiful pattern round a spiky hawthorn bush on the bank of the pool. Had she touched any of the thorns, it would certainly have torn her frail wings, but this only made her fly faster.

High above, the wind stirred the beech leaves. New sunbeams flashed down; the butterfly seemed to be winding their light among the thorns. For a few seconds she hovered, quite motionless, above the exact centre of the pond. Then she glided down towards a bright stone on the bank; but she saw, just in time, that a grey-brown, warty toad had placed his feet on it and was looking heavenwards with a pious, hungry expression. The butterfly soared upwards immediately and lighted on the highest thorn. "So that's where you've got to," she exclaimed. "You're so ugly, I tend to forget about you."

"That might be a mistake," the toad replied in a mild, though gravelly, voice. He hoisted himself onto the stone and sat for a moment, panting. "Though I have to admit," he added, "that you're probably not worth the trouble of catching. Too much air and motion in you to make a real mouthful." Without seeming to move his head, the toad darted out his long tongue and scooped up a fat black water-bug from the pool's surface. "Ugly but substantial," the toad remarked, when he could speak. "Just as I am." He burped, and added in a more kindly tone, "Of course, you only lay eggs. You imbibe no more than a drop of nectar; you only live two days. How could you have any flesh on you?"

These words didn't offend the butterfly. She darted over the dragon's back, then around his head, so that a head-shaped line gleamed in reflection on the water. "You *are* large," she remarked. "What do you do?"

These words amused Nonesuch, who was still hardly larger than a human being. "You may think I'm large now," he replied condescendingly, "but wait till I've reached my full growth."

He realized immediately that the butterfly couldn't wait; if this thought occurred to the butterfly, it didn't bother her. "What will you do *then*?" she asked.

Nonesuch wasn't sure exactly what he *would* do. He recalled the most impressive stories he had heard from his grandmother; and from his uncles too, very restless dragons who sometimes slept in the family's cavern but were always eager to be off. His uncles, he recalled, had claimed that by flying through clouds they could cut them into small pieces. "We can fly through the cloud-capped mountain peaks," he said proudly. "Nothing can stand in our way."

The other animals considered his words. "I can fly in the mist too," the butterfly said, "but it makes my wings heavy."

The turtle, who had been listening with his head submerged to his ears, now lifted it out of water. "I suppose you're going to tell us you can fly through stone," he said suspiciously.

"Of course not," Nonesuch replied. "We wouldn't want to." Though he spoke haughtily, as was always proper for a dragon, he recalled that his father and his uncles, in the zest and glory of their flights, had sometimes crashed into mountain peaks; perhaps they had imagined that the rocks would give way before them, but they never had.

The turtle's reply was even more haughty. "I should think not! All rocks are derived from the shell of the Greatest Turtle of All. Nothing can be more solid and massive!"

Before the dragon could ask him to explain this statement, the butterfly piped up again. "We don't strike against rocks, either, though we may rest on them. But the first butterfly never rested: she was a beam of light, infinitely swift. At last she grew weary of glancing off beautiful objects or passing by them, so she broke up into many butterflies. Like our ancestor, we must always keep moving."

"One certainly must avoid striking rocks," the turtle remarked ponderously.

"But we avoid nothing else!" Nonesuch asserted, not at all pleased with the way the conversation kept getting away from him. "My uncle and his cousin, Blackhearth, fought a mighty battle with the wild, uncouth, fringed dragons from the Scottish Highlands. The noise of their trumpeting shook the hills; its echoes rolled so that people couldn't sleep for a month after the battle itself. When the dragon judges declared our side the winner, the battleground had been so ploughed up that nothing grew again." His audience looked at him without speaking. "At least, not till the next year," Nonesuch conceded.

The others were silent at first. Then the toad croaked approvingly. "There must have been good rain puddles in the ploughed land afterwards: excellent places for breeding fat grubs."

"Yes!" the butterfly piped up enthusiastically, "I've seen it that way after the wild pigs have been fighting, if it rains the next day. Then we can watch our own reflections in the water, so close that they are larger than the clouds themselves."

Nonesuch didn't care at all for the comparison with wild pigs. He also recalled that it had not rained for two weeks. "How do you know about rain puddles?" he asked peevishly. "You couldn't have been alive to see it."

The butterfly was not abashed. "I've learned it from the other butterflies," she replied, as if this should have been obvious. "We tell each other everything that happens. So it's as if none of us dies at all." She darted over the dragon's back and added politely, "I'll tell them about you. Years from now the butterflies will remember that once a small dragon came to their pool."

"Well, I should think so!" Nonesuch exclaimed. "They'll be very impressed that you saw one so close; that you weren't afraid. Why, when *we* fly over a city the people scatter in fear. They run to hide in their churches and ring bells." Nonesuch glanced at the water. "They look no bigger than water-bugs then."

"Oh my!" the butterfly whistled. "I'm afraid I don't see the point of flying so high. I keep to ground level, and the children run out to catch me. Some think I'm a sunbeam, as if the first butterfly of all had returned. I avoid them, unless their hands seem gentle; then, I might perch on their wrists a moment."

The toad caught another water-bug. Nonesuch said to him, "I suppose children run out to see *you* pass too!"

The toad was too busy swallowing to answer right away. Then he said, very humbly, "Oh no, at best they laugh at me, which I don't mind. But they can be cruel too. I've seen a dozen of my brothers dangling by the feet from a twig, jerking like puppets. It's best to keep completely out of sight, in the cool grass of the fields."

He sighed. "But even then, there are scythes, and ploughs, and ploughmen's clogs to grind us into the earth. And besides these, besides all the accidental calamities, we make such excellent food! They all want to eat us,'' he said, glancing with mournful pride at his fat thighs. ''Snakes, weasels, fish, everyone. They prefer the frogs, who have smoother skins. But if they're hungry enough they'll make do even with my wrinkles and warts.''

The toad sighed again and looked at Nonesuch with soulful brown eyes. ''But I recall my glorious past. This lets me forget my troubles and fears, at least for a time.''

''*Your* glorious past!'' Nonesuch sputtered, then glared at the toad, unable to speak. Before he found his tongue, the toad continued. ''Of course, I have no such cosmic origins as my neighbors here. We are entirely creatures of earth. Some say the first toad arose from a lump of dried mud. What do I know of such matters? But I do remember my change of form,'' he explained, with simple, deep pride. ''Once I was only a tadpole, no more than a head, a stomach, and a tail. Then my legs grew out, and my tail fell off when it was no longer needed — no offence meant,'' he added hastily as the dragon swished his own tail in warning. The toad continued: ''And my bone structure changed too, until I was an unmistakable, complete toad. And I remember it all!

''Now, you will say, 'What of that? He changed from an insignificant tadpole to a hardly more significant toad.' But you also changed, when you were in the egg, and you too.'' Here the toad nodded at the turtle, and then at the butterfly. ''And you, when you were in the pupa, surrounded by a lovely silk wrapping. You each changed, in your special way. But none of you can remember it, except in dreams. *I* can recall all my changes. Sometimes it seems to me that if I tried hard enough I could even remember what it was like to be an egg. This is what we toads think about when we watch the moon, which, when it is full, is just the shape of an egg. In the evenings we sing together, again and again, 'We changed! We changed! We changed!' ''

The turtle and the butterfly listened respectfully to this ridiculous discourse. Even Nonesuch did not interrupt the small, ugly creature, but he had especially disliked the reference to his own life in an egg. This was a subject that dragons never mentioned: they were ashamed to think that once they had been so small and weak. He said spitefully to the turtle, ''I suppose *you* remember all the details of your past life too!''

The turtle swayed his head back and forth at the end of his long neck. ''No,'' he replied ponderously, ''I have long since accepted that my early life in an egg will remain a mystery to me. I have, if my humble and bumpy companion here will pardon me'' — he looked courteously at the toad — ''a more important concern: to come to terms with the burden I always carry, that is, my shell.'' He nodded towards the great orange-green dome at his back. ''I know it protects me from my enemies; for years, frankly, none has come to this pool who would even think of attacking me. Perhaps this shell is of no use to me, here. But, useful or not, we turtles all wear our shells in honor of the Greatest Turtle of All, of whom you have surely heard.''

He paused weightily. The dragon tried to figure out how large this Greatest Turtle of All could be. The particular turtle who was speaking was four times as broad as the lily-pad. Perhaps a greater one would be half as large as the pool itself. He could not imagine that so dull a creature could reach a greater size.

''The Greatest Turtle of All,'' the turtle continued solemnly, when he judged he had given the dragon enough time to answer, ''contains within her shell our earth, the sun, the moon, and the stars. All order is maintained inside that shell: light, winds, and seasons. Without the shell, everything would fly apart. And it must be strong indeed, because this Greatest Turtle is always under attack by a greater beast — a mad dragon, in fact, meaning no offence to you — who is the deadly enemy of all order. If he should win, if his teeth should crack the Greatest Turtle's shell, then all our universe will disappear and return to the dust from which it arose.

''But we think that, one day, the dragon will grow weary of the battle. Then his own rage and madness will destroy him. When that happens, all our own shells will fall away, and we will dance in the sunlight!''

Nonesuch listened to the turtle's outlandish story with growing anger. He thought of trying his own teeth out on the shell of this insolent amphibian, but realized that he could hardly get his mouth around the turtle's shell. Very well, when he grew larger he could return to the pool. By that time, however, his wings would be so wide that he could no longer fly through the beech forest. Besides, even if he returned on foot then, the turtle was hardly a worthy foe. At this moment it was looking at him benevolently, and a little sadly: as if it felt sorry for *him*. It clearly hadn't realized how deeply it had insulted him. Nonesuch grew angrier. He considered lashing all the water out of the pond with his tail and thus destroying the little world of these lowly creatures who were so small and weak that they had to make up ridiculous tales to give themselves some importance. He reared back, then recalled another of his grandmother's sayings: ''Don't become angry over little things: there are enough big ones.'' He turned and, in silent dignity, stalked away.

As he rustled through the forest, Nonesuch slashed down a hawthorn bush with one sweep of his tail, noting triumphantly that the thorns could not hurt him at all. He destroyed a dried anthill with one mighty sweep of his paw and was first amused, then ashamed, to see the tiny ants scurry about. He was delighted at last to find a worthy and edible foe, a wild boar fully as large as he. The boar fought well, gashing him twice with his sharp tusks before it gave up the battle and scurried to cover in a dense thorn thicket where the dragon could not follow him.

Their battle had left the ground scarred with many furrows and holes. Nonesuch swept it all level with his tail, so that no rain puddles could be formed. Then he found a clearing in the forest wide enough for him to spread his wings and fly away. He crossed the forest until he saw the pool again, then flew higher and higher until it almost vanished. Almost, but not quite. As long as daylight lasted it was still here, fixed in his sight, a piercing blue dot. He deliberately kept it in view, hovering and swooping, until the quiet dusk blotted out all the forest's details. His grandmother scolded him for returning so late to the cavern, but he never told her where he had been.

# CHAPTER III

# FAMILY MISFORTUNES

A S NONESUCH GREW OLDER, &
THE CATASTROPHES THAT
struck his own family stopped him from
thinking of the very trivial events of his
childhood. Troubles arrived at a gallop, and
his grandmother's most gloomy forebodings
came true.

The first to go was his grandfather, a
shambling, good-natured creature known
locally as the Worm of Grimsby Bog. He
had a flexible twenty-foot-long neck, ending
in a great broad head and a gaping mouth
that looked humorous, unless it was coming
right at you. He would eat anything: cattle;
horses, and sometimes, by accident, their
riders as well; droves of swine; flocks of
geese, feathers and all; even wagon-loads
of grain if nothing better offered. Nonesuch
had exchanged few words with his grandfather, who mainly used the family cavern
for sleeping off his huge meals.

At last, his appetite was his undoing.
The exasperated villagers, tired of seeing
all their goods disappear down that gigantic
maw, decided to cure the dragon's hunger
for good. A great rock in the south meadow
roughly resembled a cow, though twice the
size of any living one. After keeping all
their livestock indoors for a week to starve

the dragon, the villagers painted the rock reddish-brown and white, tied wooden horns to one end, and slapped on clay here and there to complete the disguise. When the Worm of Grimsby Bog arrived, snorting, the real cows scattered, all but one whose hoof was caught in a mole-tunnel; but she was no more than an appetizer. Then the Worm, whose hunger, when roused, was much greater than his prudence or common sense, licked his lips with a tongue as large as the staysail of a small coasting vessel, and swallowed the rock whole.

The unbelieving villagers were too busy watching the enormous bulge pass down the dragon's throat to notice the shocked and disgusted expression on his face. When the rock reached his stomach, the look of horror deepened. With an indignant squawk, the Worm of Grimsby Bog flapped his mighty wings and rose in the air, slanting this way and that as the rock rolled round in his belly. The dragon flew valiantly, sometimes descending to brush the tree-tops, rising again with incredible force till he looked no larger than a sparrow, then sinking low as the great rock reasserted itself. He flew over the village, scraping thatch from the roofs, and past the castle walls, whose archers were too busy placing bets on the flight's duration to loose their arrows. He flew past the marsh from which he took his name and finally, as if drawn by the hungry waves, out to sea. Humble fishermen watched, gaping like fish themselves, while the great shape sailed on, now majestic in the sun, though sagging at the bottom, now clumsily tilting to one side or the other, until, with a gurgling splash, it plunged into the sea and rose no more.

For many years after, the waters of that coast were unlucky. Fish shunned them. Fishermen had to journey far out into the region of fogs and killing gales for any kind of catch. Mothers would frighten naughty children with tales of the great dragon that dwelt beneath the waves, gathering its strength until it could rise in the air again. Some stories changed the cow-shaped stone to an anchor to which the beast had been tethered by a brave prince. Such versions gave more dignity to the dragon than the true story: that he had fallen victim to his own undiscriminating gluttony.

Nonesuch's father, the son of the Worm of Grimsby Bog, perished through his own appetites too, though more indirectly. He was a medium-sized black dragon with a high fringe of scales on his head, rather like a chef's cap. The peasants called him Greedyguts, which was not quite fair since he was more a gourmet than a glutton. Somehow, he had become overly fond of human food, the more ornate and fanciful the better. He would attack wagon-loads of savory game pies on their way to the castle for the pre-Lenten feast, and would often turn up his nose afterwards at the mules. Sometimes he would be seized by a desire for simpler fare: he would thrust his neck down a merchant's chimney and pull a sizzling haunch of beef right off the spit, or suck up whole kettlefuls of succulent soup. On warm, sultry days, Greedyguts, in search of a lighter repast, would appear at picnics, his widespread wings hiding the sun like a black cloud. After the picnickers had fled, aghast, the dragon would gobble up all the dainties, and sometimes the picnic baskets as well, but he would always wipe his mouth with the white ground-cloths before flying away.

He was considered more a nuisance than a disaster, and people accepted his visits with wry humor. After all, no one wants to turn every merry feast into an armed camp. But the day came when Greedyguts attacked Lady Ursula's betrothal feast in the marquee.

Ursula, oldest and only unmarried daughter of the Earl of Grimsby, was, at twenty-eight, handsome, stern-eyed, and critical. Her temper and her tongue scared suitors away. At last her harried father arranged a match with a silent, balding, widowed knight whose stunted castle in the Welsh mountains would supply his daughter with a sufficiently distant home of her own.

The betrothal feast was held on a beautiful June day. The wedding was to follow in four months, right after the harvest. On the lawn before the castle a marquee, a great tent, was set out, bleached linen on a carpet of bluebells and buttercups. It was open at the ends, and a merry breeze stirred the banners hanging inside. At one side a small orchestra of sackbuts, lutes, viols, and trombones played without pause. Facing them at a long table, the guests laughed and chatted, each talking more loudly than the others.

Lady Ursula, in a long gown whose color exactly matched the bluebells, sat at the centre of the table. She glanced from the guests to the musicians, and to her fiancé, who sat at her side, dour but unabashed, his eyes quietly calculating the value of the silver dishes and flagons.

Lady Ursula made a sign. The orchestra fell silent; most of the guests, in surprise, did so too. A roll of drums announced the main course. This was ushered in by the chief chef in his high white cap, followed by four serving-men in blue and yellow livery. Each one bore proudly on his head a great silver platter on which rested a whole roast peacock, stuffed with larks. The guests sniffed deeply and happily, then gasped with horror. They remained frozen with their mouths open. The long black neck of a dragon had entered the tent directly behind the last of the serving-men. Very gently the dragon lifted the peacock off the plate, with no more sound than the smacking of his thick lips. The serving-man, feeling his tray suddenly lighter, turned in surprise, clanging it against a tent-pole. While this note still sounded, the dragon ate the next peacock. His great head hung motionless in the marquee while he swallowed. The guests, still unable to move, dumbly watched the passage of the peacock down the dragon's throat. He ate the next one thoughtfully, in two bites.

Then, while all her guests remained frozen, Lady Ursula rose to her feet. She seized a trombone from one of the cowering musicians and fearlessly thrust it up the left nostril of the dragon just as it swallowed the last peacock.

The dragon, whose shoulders and forelegs were now inside the marquee, reared back with an indignant snort. He lifted the great tent from its moorings. The stretched linen sides bowled the musicians into a heap, and many of the guests with them. Those who could run dashed out the other side, bearing the table to the ground. Some, in panic, ran the other way, squeezing past the dragon's sides. Outside, the men-at-arms, roused at last from the hot afternoon's lethargy, began to hack at the dragon's tail with broadswords.

And now Greedyguts, as eager as any of the guests to be gone, tried to withdraw his head; but his scales had become entangled in the silk banners and his ears were snared by the horizontal support ropes. With a fierce tug he backed away. The marquee followed him, leaving Lady Ursula standing by the wreckage of her betrothal feast. Only when he was within the shadow of the forest was the dragon able to shake the tent and its banners from his neck and ears. He looked back at

Lady Ursula, and received such a glare of hatred that, burping apologetically, he slid out of sight among the trees.

Still Lady Ursula stood by her overturned table, ignoring all efforts to bring her to safety within the castle walls. Her fiancé remained at her side, looking at her with wonder and doubt. At last, as darkness was falling, Lady Ursula spoke quietly, but in a voice that precluded any argument. She would never marry him, she said, while that dragon, who had shamed her festive day, still lived.

The Welsh knight received this announcement silently. He tugged at his beard as if thinking that, all things considered, it might be better if the dragon lived a long time. Then he looked at the silver plates again, still lying on the grass amid bones and scraps of fruit, and at the rich trappings of the serving-men, who had started to clear away the debris, cast a quick eye on the castle's general air of soundness and prosperity, looked again at Lady Ursula, as if weighing up all the pluses and minuses, and nodded grimly to his beloved.

The Welsh knight took only time for some essential preparation before he carried out his promise. One crisp fall morning, Greedyguts was awakened from a sound sleep, and dreams of spicy sausages, by an extremely irritating cater-wauling. He opened his eyes, then closed them again, hoping the sound would go away. On the contrary, it grew shriller and more insistent. Greedyguts unwillingly dragged his head to the mouth of the cavern.

In the valley below stood a bandy-legged peasant squeezing a bagpipe, an instrument that the dragon had never before heard. Beside the peasant was a small, neat man in black armor, his helmet under his arm and a businesslike expression on his face. When Greedyguts's head came in sight the knight gave a signal and three red-clad musicians raised their long trumpets and blew three unharmonic notes. These sounds, and the continuing wail of the bagpipe, struck directly on Greedyguts's nerves.

It was a challenge not to be ignored. Though he was still groggy from last night's visit to the Lord Mayor's banquet, and though the cavern opened out into a narrow ravine which hampered his movements, Greedyguts sallied forth, huffing and growling as fiercely as was possible for a creature who mainly wanted to go back to sleep. He began to leap up and down, to obtain proper clearance for his wings in preparation for the great sweep downwards towards his puny foes, who continued making their dreadful noises.

The knight waved his hand again. The bagpipe and trumpets fell silent. On the hillside, men-at-arms carefully aimed two catapults and three trebuchets, whose pivoted beams were loaded with great stones. As the dragon leaped once more into the air, these stones were released. Two of them struck Greedyguts, flinging him against the high wall above his cavern's mouth. While the stones' momentum held him against the wall, the catapults hurled their man-long arrows, skewering the dragon like one of the roast oxen of which he had been so fond.

As the dragon's twisted body slipped down past the mouth of the cavern, a howl of such sorrow was heard that tears rose to the hardened soldiers' eyes; they all crossed themselves, even the Welsh knight. It was the dragon's guilty soul escaping his evil body, they thought. No one suspected it was the dragon's mother, wailing her foolish son's fall.

When his father was killed, Nonesuch was away on his "flyaround". It had long been the custom for young dragons, on reaching their full growth, to fly around the British Isles. They had done so before the Normans came, before the Vikings, and the Romans, and the Picts; back to the happy times when there were no people at all. In those days, his grandmother told him, the dragons had quite justifiably regarded all the land as their own. Swarms of them would fly along the coastline, soaring above the cliffs of Cornwall, skimming the angry waves of the Irish Sea, circling round each rocky island, seeing few other signs of life than their own wide wings.

But now, his grandmother said, dragons flew alone and were rarely out of the sight of man.

So Nonesuch had found it. On rocky mountains and in dark valleys he always sniffed the smoke of peat fires, sure signs of human life. When he swooped down to catch a deer, he realized it was already being pursued by hounds and horsemen.

He considered flying further out to sea to seek new lands until he found one with no trace of humans, but the thought of his family in the cavern drew him back. On his return, he learned all the details of his father's death.

"My son was worse than his father!" his grandmother lamented. "True, everyone has to eat, but to make such a production of it is worse than foolishness: it borders on stupidity!"

This was the last complete sentence Nonesuch heard his grandmother speak. She lapsed into her reveries again. Her rare words were disjointed. Sometimes "turtles and toads" again, which caused Nonesuch an unaccountable twinge. Or, with disgust, "the two-legged ones", by which she meant humans. Or, with a more comfortable sigh, "the warm, liquid rock", which at the time made no sense at all.

But for a time, Nonesuch was so immersed in his own thoughts that he hardly noticed his grandmother's silence. He was beginning to understand that strength and size, and even skill, were not enough, so long as humans existed in the world. It was bitter to think this just when he was reaching his prime; and at first he tried to put the idea away. Sometimes Nonesuch would zoom around furiously, just over the tops of trees, breaking their heavy branches with sweeps of his tail. Or he would carry huge rocks in his claws and drop them on the stony hillsides, to see them split and prove to himself that he was still as strong as ever. But he would look down and see, perhaps, some humble shepherds or ploughmen shaking their heads in disbelief. Then he would fly back to his cavern, feeling foolish and wasteful.

Often, when he returned, he found that his grandmother had opened the way to the tunnel behind her pile of treasure. And then, without knowing exactly when it had started, Nonesuch noticed that his grandmother was entering the tunnel completely. At first she disappeared for only a few minutes; gradually this extended to hours.

With each of her underground visits, Nonesuch's grandmother became more and more thoughtful. She would sit at the mouth of the cavern afterwards, her head hanging six feet out of its opening, her great dimmed eyes staring out at the valley and all the signs of busy human life. From time to time she would heave a thunderous sigh that caused the peasants to gaze up, surprised, into the clear sky. But she did not speak.

Then, from one of her underground trips, she did not return at all. Nonesuch waited for her anxiously. He left the cavern as little as possible, lest she come back in his absence. When he did leave, he piled brushwood over the tunnel mouth, to show him if his grandmother had left the hole and entered it again. He slept across the mouth of the tunnel in case she decided to come back at night.

All in vain. His grandmother was gone. And after a week of waiting, Nonesuch, who had never stuck so much as his nose into the tunnel, crawled down it in search of her.

The journey was easy at first. The hole was so wide that the edges of his folded wings barely touched the sides. It continued thus for some time, though Nonesuch soon realized that his grandmother's greater bulk and wingspan could not have passed so easily. Here and there he saw her scales clinging to the tunnel wall. He recalled that she had started to grow bright new scales since her first trips into the tunnel, which gave her a speckled appearance. In no time, daylight had vanished behind Nonesuch, and he continued by the light of his own eyes. The tunnel descended through chalk and limestone layers, the deposits of ancient seas. Surprised fossils of great sea monsters gazed out at him from the walls. Then came layers of harder rock, shining with flakes of gold and of quartz. He continued to find his grandmother's scales along the walls. There was no sign that she had retraced her path. She had gone on, and he must follow.

Time passed; was it hours or days? He didn't know; he seemed to have been in the tunnel forever. Nonesuch thought that the light from his eyes was becoming fainter. Was this from weariness, making his fires burn less brightly? No, rather all of the surfaces of the tunnel itself were glowing with heat. Blasts of hotter air were reaching him from the tunnel's further depths.

Nonesuch realized then that the tunnel had become a volcanic vent, leading down to the molten rock in the centre of the earth. Once, very long ago, his grandmother had told him, all the earth had bubbled like soup in a cauldron. But in time the surface had cooled and hardened. She had, he recalled, spoken of this with regret. Had she gone in search of "the warm liquid rocks" at last?

He could see that his grandmother had come this far: her scales were more abundant on the walls than before, glowing brighter than the dull rocks. He must follow her still.

But it grew hotter as he descended. Even dragons have their limits. Nonesuch had long since passed the level of heat at which a man's hair would have blazed up and his skin cracked and shrivelled. As he continued down he felt no pain, but he was invaded by a curious melting sensation, as if his skin were fusing to his flesh, as if all the cells and tissues of his body were losing their individual character and becoming one entity.

A few hours later, when the heat was so great that Nonesuch's paws began to be deformed by his own weight, he realized that if he went much further he would simply melt and flow into the tunnel's walls. Had this happened to his grandmother? Nonesuch could see no trace of her body on the walls; only scales that continued out of his line of sight, a path he could no longer follow.

He believed then, and he became more certain afterwards, that his grandmother had continued her journey to the end, into the molten lava itself. Perhaps, he thought (though this was much later), she had travelled to the source of strength of all dragons. Perhaps she would remain in the molten rock, growing larger and fiercer, until one day she would break the rock and earth above her and rise, larger than the British Isles, and destroy the world.

But, for the present, Nonesuch had to return. The tunnel was much narrower now than at the entrance. Somehow he turned around, forcing his head past his tail — a manoeuvre he would not have thought possible before — and slowly and sadly made his way to the surface.

# CHAPTER IV

# THE END OF THE GREAT DRAGON

## HUS, NONESUCH WAS LEFT IN POSSESSION OF AN EMPTY

cavern and a heap of treasure. He knew — his grandmother had told him often enough — that he was supposed to guard this treasure. It had been collected by his ancestors as far back as anyone could remember, though he himself had added nothing to it except a reliquary, a glass-and-gold box containing the dirty white bone of a saint. This had been stolen from a church together with the communion plate, then cast aside in a forest by the superstitious robbers who feared it might bring a curse on them. Nonesuch had found it, sniffed at it, recognized the gold in it, and carried it back to the cavern.

His grandmother shook her head. "Holy objects, now!" she had muttered. "Next we'll be turning this cavern into a shrine!" But she let the reliquary be added to the rest of the treasure.

At first Nonesuch did guard the family treasure. He crouched over it, snarling. Anyone entering the cavern would have found a very warm welcome. But no one came. In the world outside the cavern, they were not thinking of the dragons' hoard. A time of troubles had come.

Signs of this appeared everywhere. Mounted messengers hurried along the roads, gazing keenly on either side. Wagons travelled in groups, guarded by bands of archers. Men-at-arms skirmished in the forest glades; in open clearings mounted knights rode at each other with sword and lance. Secret bands of dark, ragged men attacked any unprotected cottages. Soon the peasants entered the castle walls, driving their herds before them. The deer in the forest, anxious and sharp-eared, fled at the slightest sound. Nonesuch found little to eat in forest or field, at best a few scrawny, quarrelsome goats, abandoned by their masters.

The dragon did not know, of course, that the year was 1460 and that these events were minor consequences of a civil war, the War of the Roses, between the great houses of York and Lancaster, whose emblems contained white and red roses, respectively. Indeed, he would have found it difficult to understand a civil war, or any war. As long as anyone could remember, dragons had settled disputes by formal duels, supervised by wise elders. Such contests were bloody but very seldom fatal – the judges stopped them first, and their verdict was never challenged. Thus, the thought of killing each other was almost completely foreign to dragons. (Nonesuch's grandmother said, "What with lightning, and rockfalls, and evil spells, and bad food, and knights who have to prove themselves, why should *we* have to kill dragons too?")

But humans had other practices, as he was now to witness. The air round the castle walls grew stale with waiting. An army marched up. A beautiful array of tents appeared, and the siege began: assaults on the walls with high ladders; rolling towers full of armed men; attempts to mine beneath the walls themselves. All were driven back. Trebuchets hurled boulders that bounced off the sturdy walls. Nonesuch dined well on the invaders' sheep when their keepers became distracted watching the progress of the siege.

But when the cannon arrived, even Nonesuch forgot the sheep to watch it. It was as thick through the middle as a tall oak, all bumpy with castings of gods and dragons and battle scenes. It lay in a wagon, drawn by six tall, stout horses with bored, heavy-lidded eyes. The castle's defenders lined the walls to watch it come and cheered when it paraded past, just out of arrow range. But they did not cheer long.

The cannon's first shot tore out a wooden bridge that connected a tower to a wall; the next cracked the tower itself. A third blew a hole in the thick, iron-bound drawbridge. The besiegers advanced with scaling-ladders. But as they approached, the broken drawbridge dropped, still sound enough for a troop of soldiers to sally forth; obviously, more of them than the besiegers had expected. A grim battle began outside the walls, in which the men of the castle seemed well able to take care of themselves.

After watching these practices of the humans for some time from within the forest, Nonesuch wandered away, deep in thought. He had seen the trebuchets, which must have been like those that had tossed his father around so easily. The new, noisy weapon was obviously much more powerful still. Now the cannon fired again. Nonesuch turned back and saw the ball bounce off the wall and smash into a siege tower, splitting it and spilling out soldiers like ants from an anthill.

He decided not to watch any more. In a short time the besiegers and the besieged paused to stare at his wide wings cleaving the air as the dragon flew away into the cloudy sky. He stayed aloft all day, till his strength was almost exhausted, looking at the changing cloud shapes below, as if they could describe how the world had changed.

So Nonesuch did not see what actually happened at the castle. He did not see the cannon, loaded beyond its capacity in an attempt to breech the wall, explode and kill the gun crew, half a dozen knights who had gathered round to watch, and three of the horses. But even if he had seen this, it would not have altered the firm judgement he reached during his flight: that the days of dragons as great, powerful beasts were numbered. That, no matter how big and strong a dragon was, the humans could make something bigger, or at least stronger.

Nonesuch's scales bristled as this came home to him. His flight was slowed, and he almost flipped over in the air. For one glorious moment, he thought of facing the cannon below and dying nobly in combat. Then he remembered the force of the cannon-balls. Humans might cast themselves vainly against unbeatable odds. This seemed to be their nature, his grandmother had said with disgust. But their ways were not his. Here was a new problem, and there was no one to guide him. What would he do?

While thinking of this, Nonesuch flew in great sweeps above the earth. Below, fearful people pointed to heaven and crossed themselves. They were sure that, in these evil times, a flying dragon was a portent of yet more evil days to come.

And Nonesuch looked down on the earth too: on the tiny huts of the peasants; on the castle, which from this height was no bigger than his toenail; on the besieging troops which resembled wood-lice. He widened the circle of his flight. He soared westward, over the great beech forest, unchanged since his childhood. At one instant a round blue pool winked up at him, but he thought, proudly, that he was far too big and far too wise to fly down amid the trees. He flew north. The city of

Salisbury appeared below; the spire of its cathedral, already two hundred years old and weathered with time, seemed no bigger than a scrub pine. As long as he stayed high above the earth, humans and their works seemed puny enough. But he could not stay up there forever, looking down on them. He had to see to his treasure. Thoughtfully, Nonesuch glided back to his hill and into his cavern.

A glance showed him that the treasure was still undisturbed. But Nonesuch regarded it with a feeling of strangeness. It had looked familiar and comforting when his grandmother spread herself over it, so that the pieces of gold made patterns on her patterned scales. Or when his father or his grandfather had slept off their feasts in the cavern. They had always seemed more comfortable if their bellies rested on the treasure heap — and they scattered the coins about with their sleepy twisting and writhing so that his grandmother had to sweep them back with her tail in the morning.

Once, Nonesuch remembered, after she had put the pile into particularly good order, she told him again, ''Always guard your treasure!'' But then, after a time, she had added, ''Remember, be as light on your feet as on your wings. A wise dragon is always poised for departure.''

''But Grandmother,'' Nonesuch could not help protesting after he had thought over these words, ''how will I guard my treasure then?''

''That you must decide for yourself,'' his grandmother replied haughtily. And then, to preclude any further argument, ''Consistency is a human virtue, of little account to a dragon.''

Nonesuch thought of his grandmother's words. He thought so long that darkness fell, then another day passed, and darkness fell again while he crouched motionless. When day broke again, he rose stiffly and thrust his head into the tunnel, behind the heap of treasure. Then he withdrew his head, turned to the treasure heap, and filled his mouth with coins.

It was hard work, the hardest he had ever done or heard of: he carried the treasure down into the tunnel, the coins and jewels in his mouth, the shields and his one reliquary balanced on his back, between his wings. He went almost as far as he had gone before into the tunnel, and it took three trips, or perhaps four, for at the end he had lost count. He made one last trip to be sure that no fragments of treasure had been left along the way to tempt adventurers to go further. Now he was certain that he had brought the treasure to a part of the tunnel so hot that no humans could live. Before he returned for the last time to the world outside, he spoke into the glowing darkness of the tunnel's depth, ''There, Grandmother, I've brought all the treasure to you. Guard it well.''

He spent another day staring at the mouth of the tunnel. Then he piled all the loose boulders in the cavern into its entrance and fetched others from the hillside until the entrance was sealed off. No human would now suspect that the tunnel existed. Even though Nonesuch knew that the heat would kill any men who approached the treasure, he wanted to keep them as far away as possible.

Now, he thought, he was indeed a dragon without a treasure. Perhaps he had no more dignity than a turtle or a toad – or even a butterfly. But, since there were no members of his family left to mock such simple creatures, he did not feel inclined to do so either.

 In the world outside, the siege of the castle continued. The defenders valiantly drove the enemy away again; then they were defeated by treachery when a disaffected knight let the besiegers in at night through a secret gate. The castle was taken, and destroyed.

All that could be burned was burned, and the walls were blasted away with gunpowder. Nonesuch watched from greater and lesser distances, gliding through the maze of caverns in his hill, flying out at night – for at this time, he felt it more seemly not to show himself – to survey the scene at dawn from a distant vantage point. And now the castle had stopped smoking; a few scorched and meagre peasants were setting up huts in the shadow of its ruined walls.

During all this time, Nonesuch ate very little. In fact, he had eaten nothing since removing the treasure; but strangely, he did not feel hungry. His stomach didn't shrink, as it used to do when food was scarce. In the past, even if his insides didn't tell him so, he had always known it was time to eat when, without craning his neck, he could see his large hind toe with its gold nail, normally hidden by the swell of his belly. But now his toe didn't appear at all. He had to crane his head to see it; and he did this so often his neck became sore.

Nonesuch realized the cause of this curious change when he stopped to scratch his back against a sharp rock ridge with a hook-like projection that, in the past, had just fit his shoulder. Now he felt nothing. He looked back: it seemed that the hook was a foot higher than it used to be! Not believing his own eyes, he next compared the size of his foot to that of his footprint, dried in the mud at the cavern's threshold from a rainy spell two weeks before. He measured the length of his tail by dangling it over the ledge before his cavern's mouth. Before, his tail would reach exactly down to the forest floor; he knew this from the many times he had hung it over that ledge to beat out the twigs caught in the scales, for Nonesuch was a tidy beast. All these measurements confirmed that he had shrunk proportionately all over.

Nonesuch soon decided that he had changed because he

had not been eating. He was able to test this quickly: though most of the regular flocks had been eaten or driven away, the wild boars had become bolder and were roaming out of the forest and invading former pasture-land. Nonesuch had some good chases and some delicious meals afterwards on the gamy flesh. His long fast had not weakened him. On the contrary, he found that he hunted with more vigor, that he was more agile for being smaller. After he ate, he grew again. And when he stopped, he shrank. He took his measurements carefully: there was no possibility of a mistake.

What could have caused this? We will never know for certain, but in time Nonesuch became convinced that the great heat to which he had been exposed while following his grandmother down the tunnel had worked a change in all his tissues, so that their overall dimensions altered with his food supply. As far as we know, he was the only dragon to whom this happened, for no other dragon went so close to the molten rock at the core of the earth, and then returned in a fleshy form.

But Nonesuch found that as he grew smaller, he grew livelier, more alert. It wasn't only his fighting skill that improved: the air tasted better, colors looked brighter, he breathed more quickly and thought more quickly too.

He had already come to the conclusion that there was little profit in being a very big dragon. Now, he realized, nothing stopped him from becoming a small one. Perhaps then he would find the world more to his taste.

Since neither hunger nor weakness troubled him when he went without food, he decided to forgo eating altogether; just a quick snack now and then so he wouldn't forget how. Otherwise, he would continue fasting until he reached a size that really suited him.

# CHAPTER V

# A POOL IN THE FOREST

W HAT A STRANGE IDEA, YOU WILL SAY:  WHAT A DIS-grace for a dragon to *choose* to grow smaller! At first it appeared so to Nonesuch himself. A short way into his change, he did not seem to fit into any dignified description at all. He was just a large dragon, still the largest creature around, but smaller than he should be, considering his age. If he had not been even more obstinate than most dragons, he would have eaten his fill and grown again. But, once having started to grow smaller, he was unwilling to stop until he saw a clear reason to do so.

When he was only fifteen feet long, Nonesuch became aware of his first source of danger. His cousin, Cauchemar, began eyeing him with unusual interest. Cauchemar's eyes shone and his mouth watered unpleasantly. He had always turned up in unexpected places before, but now this seemed to be happening more often. When Nonesuch was only two-thirds the length of his cousin, Cauchemar became bolder. Till now, he had kept strictly to his own side of the hill and had never entered Nonesuch's family cavern. He still did not cross the cavern's threshold, but he waddled or slithered past it every day, more slyly arrogant each time.

Nonesuch began to suspect that his cousin was planning to add cannibalism — and of a close relative at that! — to his other crimes. But the violent times prevented this from happening.

Since the destruction of Grimsby Castle, social order had almost disappeared from the surrounding world of men. Small groups of peasants huddled together in clusters of brushwood huts, guarding themselves and their flocks as best they could with crude weapons and farm implements. Around them ranged bands of cruel brigands, some of whom were waiting for the harvest before they descended on their prey. Sometimes the peasants would call for help from travelling homeless knights or men-at-arms. They would exchange food and goods for protection. But the character of the "protectors" was such that, as one chronicler of the times wrote, "The poore sheepe did not knowe whych was worse, the shepherdes or the wolves."

In the ruins of the castle itself now lived a robber band named "The Undergrowthe". Led by the bold, hard-drinking Black Miles, they specialized in robbing travellers on the way to the coast from Salisbury. There was good business here, since at this time many of the more prosperous townspeople were trying to resettle abroad, or in the Isle of Wight, which was still relatively peaceful.

The robbers had put together enough stores and weapons to protect them from any of the human enemies that had appeared thus far. But in their sorties and forays, they exposed themselves sufficiently to provide many tasty meals for Cauchemar. Though they tried, in a simple-minded fashion, to avoid the wily dragon, their cruel, twisted thoughts and schemes drew him surely towards them. When they spied the mud-colored dragon lurching away with a look of sly satisfaction on his face, the men of The Undergrowthe could be sure that their number had been reduced by at least one more.

The clerk of the band was named Ambrose, sometimes "Brother Ambrose" because of his pious demeanor. He was the only one of the group who had been born in the village of Serpent Grimsby. He had served as altar-boy in the church and later as pot-boy in the tavern. He had known of the dragon since his own childhood; thus far, he had avoided any of the places where Cauchemar might hunt. Since he knew that evil thoughts attracted the dragon, he mixed his ill deeds with thoughts of higher things. His comrades were sometimes shocked to see Brother Ambrose, his dagger and clothing splashed with blood, walk along with pious steps, reciting lengthy prayers. He also remembered the dragon's taste for alcoholic beverages, or rather for those who consumed them.

Brother Ambrose reflected long on the dragon's nature while he sat with his book of records in his accustomed place, behind his bold captain and equally bold lieutenant, the one-legged "Lopped Cedric". Ambrose's fresh, smooth face was sorrowful, his blue innocent eyes almost weeping as he recorded the loss of yet another member of the band. From one of their raids he hid a small cask of rare fortified Rhenish wine, for later use.

A month afterwards, the captain and the lieutenant returned from another raid, leading a pack-train of goods from which all the guardians had fled. Only the fat cook and a slim, pretty kitchen wench remained, tied together on one of the mules. The cook was howling with indignation, the girl was pale with fear. The clerk brought the wine cask out to the victorious warriors and volunteered to lead the mules with their burden of treasure into the ruined castle walls. He also suggested, winking, that he relieve them of the company of the cook, who could be better employed making supper for the band.

Brother Ambrose stopped to watch the two heroes break open the wine cask and begin to toast each other and the girl with their silver flagons. Then he continued on to the castle. Once inside he saw that the spoils were safely stowed away. He mildly but firmly discouraged any of the others from joining the captain and the lieutenant, who, he said, had quite enough company as it was. The fat cook wailed and lamented. The clerk, bowing in mockery, handed her a great kitchen ladle. She looked at the ladle, then grasped it firmly. She used it to clear away a robber who was sleeping in the cold fireplace. She chased two robbers out to get more wood, made another sweep the floor, and soon had cooked them their first decent meal in months. Brother Ambrose fetched some more wine, almost as good as that which he had given to the heads of the band. He insisted that they take time to savor it properly. So that, when he finally led the men outside with pinewood torches to join their leaders, he found what he had expected: a large, mud-colored dragon with huge shining eyes that dropped giant tears as he listened to the melodious lamentations of the innocent kitchen girl, who was tethered by one foot to a tree. Of the captain and the lieutenant nothing was to be seen, except the hand of the former, too laden with rings to be digestible, and Lopped Cedric's wooden leg.

The dragon was quite drunk. His sighs resembled an old drinking song; their sound convinced the superstitious robbers that their two leaders were still singing in the dragon's belly. Some fled, others fell on their knees and crossed themselves. Only the clerk kept his presence of mind. He ran back to the ruined castle for two small barrels of gunpowder, which he placed beneath the dragon's wings. In doing this, he gained great respect from the rest of the band, who didn't know, as he did, that the dragon, when intoxicated, remained motionless for hours. The clerk unpegged the kitchen wench, called the band back to a safe distance, laid a train of gunpowder to the barrels, and dropped an ember at the far end of the train. As the explosion blasted the dragon into three pieces, the amazed robbers saw his eyes light up, just for an instant, with fierce joy at this new experience.

This episode was the true beginning of Brother Ambrose's career. After his chief rival for the post was found floating in a pond one dark night, Ambrose was unanimously elected leader of The Undergrowthe. He directed it with great success. The band became more respectable and hired out as mercenaries. Eventually Ambrose joined the winning side in the civil war. As a reward, he was later given the castle for his own, money to rebuild it, and a noble title.

And while all these events, of greater or less importance in human history, were taking place, Nonesuch continued to shrink.

For some time he was still the largest creature in the vicinity. He judged it wiser to keep out of human sight as much as possible. He flew mostly at night; people seeing his silhouette against the moon could easily believe he was as large as ever. No one realized he was growing smaller, except for children, who whispered about it among themselves; but who cared what *they* thought? Nonesuch began to find the night a more comfortable time to be abroad. He would stay aloft, or sometimes perch in the highest trees until shortly before sunrise, when he would fly back to his cavern.

One bright moonlit night, he found the contours of the beech forest over which he was flying strangely familiar. Though it made him uneasy to do so, he lighted on a tree and waited until dawn broke. Yes, directly beneath him was the same round blue pool he had seen in his childhood.

By this time Nonesuch, though much older, was almost the same size as when he had first visited the pool. He flew down between the trees. This time, he realized, he was much more skilled in flying and could zoom between the branches in an elegant and daring fashion. Even the butterfly would be impressed to see such flying from a dragon, he thought; though of course the butterfly was long dead.

He landed by the pool's brim. The hawthorn bush on the bank had grown; there were two lily-pads where one had been before. At first there was no other sign of life on the pool's surface, except for a line of skating water-bugs. Then a turtle's head broke water, a wrinkled head with wise eyes that peered keenly at the dragon.

"So," the turtle remarked after a time, "you've learned some manners. Now you wait before you stick your nose in." He cleared his eyes by dipping his head in the water and looked at the dragon again. "You're older, but no larger. How is that?"

"I was larger before; now I'm growing smaller," Nonesuch told him modestly.

"Extraordinary!" the turtle remarked. "Can you stop growing smaller?"

"If I like," the dragon replied. "So far, I haven't found the proper size."

"You're not a bad size now, especially since you've lost some of your youthful bumptiousness." The turtle swam around the pool, always keeping his eyes on the dragon, regarding him from different perspectives.

"He flies very well!" a shrill voice remarked.

"For his size, he's hardly clumsy at all," said a second shrill voice. Two butterflies skimmed the surface of the pool, their bright-yellow wings almost touching.

"They told us all dragons were awkward in the air," the first butterfly said.

"Because of their size," said the second.

"But you seem to have caught on to the knack of flying," the first added. Nonesuch looked down modestly and saw in the water the reflection of the two butterflies, who flew in a circle round his head until he grew dizzy watching them.

"What happened to the toad?" he asked.

The turtle shook his head. "A hopeful but unlucky creature," he replied. "A snake caught him."

"That's a pity," Nonesuch remarked, surprising himself.

"It was years ago," the turtle said. "*I* ate the snake later, though usually I'm a vegetarian; there's all the nutrition you need in water weeds, really. But now, in a sense, I can speak for the toad too." He frowned thoughtfully. "Ever since I absorbed the rest of him, along with the snake, I've become much more aware of the changes within my own body. I can feel my shell thickening, infinitesimally, as I grow older. Where the skin of my neck rubs off against my shell, I can feel it growing again. What it must be to live as a toad! But speaking for both of us, we would be happy if you chose to stay here.''

''Oh yes!'' the butterflies piped up together, ''a dragon of our own!''

''You want me to stay here?'' Nonesuch asked in a surprised but pleased voice.

''Indeed yes,'' the turtle replied. ''It would add a touch of distinction to our little pool.'' Seeing the dragon's look of wonder, he added, ''Dragons have often been associated with water: one of their traditional roles is to guard springs. Many large lakes have their own dragon to watch over them. You, for example, might make your lair over the spring that feeds this pool, just there beneath the yew trees.'' He nodded. ''Also, you could lurk around the perimeter of the pool itself, make threatening displays on occasion, fly over it from time to time, now that you can fly so well.''

Nonesuch looked round the quiet forest glade, over the fresh cool surface of the pool. He sniffed the shady air, full of woodland odors. There was plenty of game all about, he knew, should he wish to stay by the pool and keep his present size.

The turtle added, ''I have a more selfish reason for wanting you to stay here. I think that we are in danger. Humans often come here. At one time we never saw any from one year to the next. Now they arrive in bands. They water their horses in the pool – fat, juicy horses,'' he added slyly.

The butterflies, who had trustingly perched on Nonesuch's head, one behind each ear, spoke up together. ''They build their fires among the trees and leave the ground all scorched and black. They scatter their waste everywhere. Disgusting!''

''I understand, from their talk, that times are hard out there in their own world,'' the turtle continued. ''Apparently they think that gives them the right to trespass on our property. They've even put fishing lines into our pool; not that there are any fish worth catching. But I have to keep out of sight: they might take a fancy to make soup out of me. If only there were a dragon near the pool, they'd keep well away from us.''

''A dragon of our own!'' the butterflies repeated, more excited than before. Their shrill voices tingled in Nonesuch's ears. ''We'd spread the word, and all the other butterflies would come: blue, and green, and black ones with white eyes on their wings. We'd fly in a wreath around your head! We'd bring you word of everything and everyone in the forest!''

''Including the humans,'' one butterfly added. ''But they'd keep away.''

''It would be beautiful and peaceful,'' put in the other. ''Except that a knight could come to fight you.''

''They do, you know,'' the first butterfly said.

''Then we'd see such a battle!'' cried the second.

''Which you'd win, of course.''

''And the other knights would come for the body of their comrade.''

''And carry it away, very solemnly.''

''At night.''

''With candles burning, like golden butterflies.''

''And never come back again.''

Then both butterflies said together, ''It would be lovely!''

The prospect excited Nonesuch too; for a moment he swished his tail, as if one of those valiant knights were now before him. He thought, briefly, that it was all very well for the butterflies to imagine such a gallant scene: they wouldn't be alive to see if it really happened. For himself, he might be willing to take a chance on this future, as the guardian dragon of the spring. But then he realized that by accepting the offer of these friendly creatures he would be turning back from the adventure he had set himself in becoming smaller, which might be the greatest adventure of all. Besides, though he hardly liked to admit it, he was finding the world outside, the world of humans, too interesting to leave it completely.

"No, I can't stop now," he said regretfully, at last. "I must grow smaller still. I have to continue: how much further, I still don't know."

The turtle nodded gravely. Nonesuch was grateful to him for not attempting to change his mind. "But I may come back one day," he added, thinking that, since he could always grow larger at will, he could still return to this pool, if he chose it out of all the world.

"We'll always be glad to see you, in whatever size," said the turtle. And the butterflies cried, "Oh yes, if you were small enough we could play with you. We could *really* teach you how to fly!"

Nonesuch let this last remark pass. He walked away from the pool, thinking that if he stayed much longer, he would stay forever. He flew off into the highest trees, waiting for dusk before he returned to his cavern, where he still slept.

 Now Nonesuch's size began to decrease more quickly. In a few weeks he was no larger than a fullgrown mastiff, though much stronger and a much better fighter. He came to know this in an encounter with the black hound Féroce, who guarded the bed of Brother Ambrose after he assumed the leadership of The Undergrowthe. So far, Féroce had killed one prospective assassin and crippled another. In the daytime he wandered about the forest to keep order there. Seeing a strange new creature, slightly smaller than himself, he advanced to the attack, grim and silent. In a minute Féroce was in wild retreat; he fled to the castle for shelter, yipping and howling in terror at this flying thing that could bite and slash from any direction.

For a moment the excitement and pride of battle raised Nonesuch's hunger again. Perched on an oak branch, he licked the blood from his teeth and looked thoughtfully after the fleeing black and bloody dog. Should he finish the battle properly and eat him? Then Nonesuch shook his head. Let the beaten animal go and heal its wounds, if it could. It was no contest now: Nonesuch would see what he could do when he was smaller still, perhaps with the same dog.

He was not to have the chance. Brother Ambrose had become very fastidious. He insisted that his surroundings be perfect, his clothing without spot, the manners of his table servers polished. When the tattered Féroce limped into his presence, the dog read his own death warrant in Brother Ambrose's cold eye. He fled faster than he had from the little dragon and never returned.

Two months later, when Nonesuch was the size of a cat, he learned very well what he could do when he was smaller. Féroce's brother, the white-and-liver-spotted Grimace, who was accustomed to guard the outer walls of the ruined castle, challenged the green-winged creature that had perched insolently on the coat of arms of the late Earl of Grimsby above the main portal: a stone griffin above two crossed lances. Nonesuch, who had simply been enjoying the sun-warmed stone, descended to do battle. Disdaining to take advantage of his wings, he fought entirely on the ground. Even so, his movements were so much swifter than those of Grimace, his teeth and claws so sharp, that the astounded dog soon backed away through a hole in the broken wall, howling dolefully. After this, Grimace took care only to attack creatures larger than himself, and became a superb and noted watchdog.

Meanwhile, Nonesuch flew to his perch again and crouched below the griffin, looking up at it as if for approval. The base of the coat of arms protruded enough to shield him from the sight of any humans directly below. The stones of the shady wall were green with moss, so that he could not easily be seen from farther away. He stayed there, growing smaller still, until peace brought workmen to repair the castle gates. These workmen also tore down the stone griffin and set up the new coat of arms of Brother Ambrose, now Sir Ambrose: a fierce weasel rampant on two foolish-looking sheep.

Nonesuch returned to the forest, fasting as before. He continued to grow smaller. And the smaller he became, the more fierce and savage did he find the world around him. When he was the size of a large rat, he was able to conquer a wild, starved tomcat, but it was a hard fight. His foe was able to leap as well as he, and Nonesuch's wings gave him little advantage; though finally the cat made a snarling retreat.

Nonesuch found that his own courage grew as he became smaller: perhaps it was all the courage of a great dragon now concentrated in his tiny body. Sometimes, it was true, he felt curiously empty. At first he thought this was due to hunger, but the feeling was different: as if nothing now tied him to the world around him. He puzzled over this at times, then decided, without understanding why, that it must be a feeling natural to anyone who became smaller.

When his size approached that of large insects, Nonesuch began to eat these insects so that he would not grow any smaller. It was the ways of the insects themselves (except for the butterflies) that made him decide to keep his size. He did not want to be like them in any way. He was not ashamed of his horror at their cold eyes with so many separate lenses, their expression of cold ferocity. Their fighting habits seemed too sneaky to him, not really worthy of a proper animal. Many had poisoned fangs. Others could lay their eggs in, or shoot them into, the bodies of other insects, so that the eggs would hatch there and devour their hosts from within. One of these creatures even tried spraying its eggs at Nonesuch, but they bounced off his scales. He ate his opponent, and its eggs as well, and resolved to grow no smaller. Let the insects fight each other, in their own way: he would stick to foes with more dignity! There were quite enough of these now.

All the changes in his life did not involve bloody adventures. Word had gone out among the birds that this new green bird — as they thought — was not to be trifled with, but that he was not dangerous if you let him alone. He shone so in the sunlight that many of the more agile birds began to play with him, flying close and round about him, as if he were really one of their own. On one especially gusty day, when fine, stinging dust filled the air, Nonesuch realized the true difference between the birds and himself. He had taken shelter from the dust in the lee of an exposed boulder at the top of a steep hill. The birds stayed in the air; the wind whirled them about like dried leaves or snowflakes. Such light, fragile creatures they were! They seemed to move almost as fast as the dust grains, so that the dust hardly stung them. Whereas he, a dragon, however small, was so much more solid and heavy, even in the air. He was not the air's plaything: he made his own way through it. He might envy the birds' ease and lightness, but he also thought of them condescendingly: of course they were light, they had no treasure.

Then a voice spoke within him: Neither have you!

Nonesuch stayed motionless on the rock, while the light birds soared crazily in the tumultuous wind. They whirled high above him, watching with interest this shiny spot of green on the rock — for the sun had come out though the wind was as high as ever – this spot that didn't budge for hours, as if it too were stone.

What was a treasure, after all? Nonesuch asked himself. Though his body didn't move, his mind leaped and searched the past. He pictured the treasure back in the cave: all the piles of coins, the jewels, the halberds inlaid with gold and ivory. When he was very young indeed, when he had first realized that this large pile of objects, not all of them beautiful, was a "treasure", something to be kept and increased, he had wondered why. He remembered, now, his grandmother talking to his grandfather, the Worm of Grimsby Bog, who was so full of his dinner of a herd of prize white cows that he could scarcely keep his eyes open. "What do *we* want it for?" his grandmother asked. "We treasure the things because humans do. And how did *they* get it? Better not to ask. Why should *we* want it?"

This woke the Worm up. "It's treasure, my dear," he said, mildly but firmly, and fell asleep again.

Then Nonesuch heard his grandmother mutter, "The worst of it is, he's right! A dragon without treasure has part of his soul missing: his heart is hollow." These words seemed to resonate in Nonesuch's heart now, though he was sure his grandmother had added in a very low voice, "And we care for these things only because humans do!"

Nonesuch stirred on his rock as he remembered these words; above, the birds twittered excitedly. He thought he had rid himself of his family's treasure easily when he became small. But apparently he had not lost the need of one. He could not go back to the old treasure again: he could not bring it back to the surface, and if he did, he could never guard it. But the thoughts of the treasure, and his family lying among it, brought him back to the cavern again that windy evening.

It was no longer empty. Firelight flickered on the arched stone walls. Smoke drifted out of the entrance; Nonesuch flew through it and perched on a dark ledge. A herd of sheep covered the cavern's floor like a dirty black-and-white carpet. Against the pile of stones by the old entrance to the tunnel two shepherds sat over a fire. "Fetch us another log, Dickon," the larger one said.

The smaller man reached over and pulled a log from beneath a sleeping ewe, who baa'd indignantly. "They say a dragon lived here once," he remarked. "And watched over his treasure."

The larger shepherd lifted a leather bottle to his mouth. "A likely story!" he said at last. "He never would have left it."

The sheep baa'd together, as if they agreed with these words. Nonesuch looked at the whole sleepy crew of them, wondering if a few bites would stir them up. It hardly seemed worth it. He rose and flew out into the night.

Soon he was high in the air, as high as when he had been a great dragon silhouetted against the moon. He flew in one wide circle at first, keeping the cavern in view by the glow of firelight in its entrance. When the trees hid this from sight, he continued, high and lonely in the air. In the dawn, after a long and weary flight, he was perched on a tree in the beech forest. He must be above the pool, he thought, though he could only see a small crescent of brown water. Possibly it was a rain puddle, left from the wild boars' battles. The pool must be elsewhere, not far away. Nonesuch waited until full daylight to descend. Even then he did not go to the pool at once, but skimmed here and there in descending sweeps, as if to reconnoitre a land that would be his new home. All night, as he flew, he had thought of the wise turtle's wish that he guard the pool. A year had passed since he had last visited it. Now it must be time to stay there: to eat and grow and keep the pool and its inhabitants from harm.

But when he saw, unmistakably, the hawthorn bush at the pool's rim, Nonesuch knew it could never again be as it was. There were gaps in the vegetation on either side of the bush. Two strange brown sticks projected in the air. These, when he flew closer, proved to be the hind legs of a dead horse. The horse's body lay in the pool, atop the body of its rider, of whom only the legs could be seen. Green and blue trousers, red leather on the stirrup, and long pointed golden shoes, now all sadly discolored, proclaimed that the rider had been a gallant squire.

Other things had been tossed in the pool, too: a tent, also slashed, one banner still waving brightly above the water; two broken, submerged barrels; a wagon wheel; a small ladder; a coil of scorched rope. These objects covered the surface of the pond; much of the water had drained off elsewhere. Nonesuch flew quickly over the ruined pond, glad at least not to see signs of the turtle or of any other living creature, except for a host of buzzing flies. There must be some story behind all these objects, he knew, but it seemed hardly worth while to learn it.

A quick spot of sunlight flashed at him from high in the trees. It was a butterfly, descending to see him closer.

Nonesuch perched on the hawthorn bush, which hardly stirred beneath his weight. The butterfly circled round him ten times, then lighted on a thorn. "Oh, you are a dragon!" it said in a shrill, melancholy voice.

"Why did you come?" Nonesuch asked.

"Only to see you," the butterfly replied. "We don't visit the pool now. Once, they said a dragon had come and would come again to protect it. For a moment I thought it was you, come too late. But you're much smaller than the last dragon. I never even heard of such a small dragon as you are now.'' The butterfly began to circle higher and the spirit in its voice lifted. ''Come with me to the meadow; we live there now,'' it invited Nonesuch.

But the thought of playing among the butterflies tempted Nonesuch only for a moment: they were such creatures of the air that to live with them would be like turning into air himself. He must leave the pond, and the forest as well, and never think of returning. There was no reason now to come back.

He thanked the butterfly politely, and flew away; the butterfly accompanied him to the tops of the beeches before turning back. Nonesuch continued out of the forest in a rising wind that sped him along. He was very careful not to look down, lest he see any trace of where the pool had been.

# BROTHER THEOPHILUS

HE WIND HAD RISEN WHILE
NONESUCH WAS IN THE
forest. Now it was stronger than he had
ever remembered it. Even when he was still
among the trees it reached for him, blowing
him near the branches. He flew above the
highest trees and spread his wings to ride
along the moving air. A swarm of torn,
flying leaves followed him in a green cloud
as he was blown out of the forest and over
country he had never seen before. Without
any effort of his own, he passed over a
small village that did not seem to have been
damaged in the human wars. The wind was
lifting the thatch from the roofs. One wattled
house was on fire, burning brightly, as if
the flames wanted to escape into the sky
too.

The wind never slackened. Nonesuch
was carried over a leafless apple orchard,
where bright apples were being blown from
the boughs. He flew past the round tower
of a squat castle. He soared over a group of
low grey stone buildings surrounded by a
lower grey stone wall. The last, and tallest,
of the buildings, still within the wall, was a
narrow but lofty church. The wind paused
suddenly, then with a quick puff deposited
Nonesuch gently on the glass of a high
window at the end of the church's nave.

He had landed between two upright strips of stone on a slab of colored glass, held in place by strips of iron. The wind's pressure increased again, forcing him against the dark glass. He pushed himself back, but the wind would not let him fly away. Then Nonesuch realized he was not alone on the window: across the next rib of stone was a small brown bat, upside down and apparently fast asleep. Nonesuch could see its little pig's snout and sharp white teeth. The bat, who was breathing quite peacefully, seemed fastened to the glass by the pressure of the wind. Then, when the wind dropped again, he started to slide down. He reached out a winged arm, somehow seized one of the stone ribs, worked himself down to a crack where the glass had come away from its metal frame, and squeezed through. In a moment, Nonesuch also flapped down to the hole in the window and followed the bat inside the church.

The swift clouds that had covered the sun until now suddenly broke away from it. On the inner side of the window, Nonesuch found himself flying in a wonderful world of light. Colors shone all around him. In astonishment he flew away from the window until the spots of color that composed it gathered themselves together.

The window was made up of twelve oblong frames, each of which contained a man in a long robe. Wide gold rings circled their heads. One of the men held a great gold key in his hand. Another man held an open book, another a fisherman's net, yet another a carpenter's square. Each figure had solemn features and dark, shining eyes, which seemed to look directly at him.

Nonesuch hovered in the air, staring back at these twelve men. Then he felt the emptiness of the church behind him and turned away from the window to look down the nave, the main aisle. It was dim, shadowy, with rays of colored light entering from other windows at the sides. At the far end, past the altar, a circular rose window filled the upper wall. Nonesuch flew towards it, over the empty benches of the congregation, and lighted on a high wrought-iron screen that separated the choir and altar from the rest of the church. On each side of the choir were two rows of seats, separated by richly carved partitions. Before every three seats was a small table, on which lay what seemed to be a pack of brown leather, about two feet square.

A distant bell rang; another nearer one answered it. There was the sound of feet. From the far end of the church a double file of monks, each in a long black cloak, paced down the nave, chanting more or less together. They passed under the screen, and each took his place in the choir. A few peasants entered the church behind them.

While the monks continued to sing, a short and rotund monk climbed the stairs to a pulpit on the right side of the screen. Nonesuch realized that if any of these monks looked up, they could see him. He quietly sidled to the edge of the screen, which ended at one of the columns that supported the roof, leaped out, and, in the shelter of the column, flew up to its capital, a wide stone platform two-thirds of the way up. Above this platform the column soared upward, dividing into many ribs of white stone that flowed up to the roof like a stone fountain. Nonesuch gazed up in wonder: the spread-out stone seemed to float there, as if the roof were holding it in the air.

A voice spoke directly at his feet. ''It's called 'fan vaulting'. One of the characteristics of Perpendicular Gothic, if you'd like to know. Human beings are often as much affected by it as you are.''

Nonesuch had leaped into the air as soon as the voice spoke. He flew away from the column, then turned and hovered just below the capital. The lower part of the platform was decorated with carved stone faces that looked down into the church. Between the faces were carved bunches of grapes and plums. The brown bat was there too, hanging upside down, his feet gripping a carved branch, slowly chewing on a fat moth.

The bat swallowed, licked his lips, and looked up at the dragon. "When the light from the Heaven window strikes the stone fruit, the insects think it's real. See." He pointed with one wing, and Nonesuch saw that a shaft of glorious blue light from a high window had made the stone plum glow like a real one.

"But I have to be careful," the bat added. "On other columns some of the fruit has insects carved as well. I've chipped my teeth on them."

Below them, the chanting stopped for a moment. As if on a signal, every third monk in the choir bent over, seized the corner of one of the packs of brown leather, and flung it back. In an instant, eight large books, each four feet wide and two feet high, lay open before the monks in the choir. Three read from each book as they chanted the responses.

Nonesuch had never seen or heard of a book before. It seemed to him as if light were shining out of the pale vellum pages. He looked at the rich black letters and the decorations between them with deep attention. To see them more closely, he flew below the capital, peeking round its end to get a better view.

The bat opened one eye and looked out at him. Nonesuch landed on the top of the capital again. "If you're really interested in such things," the bat told him, "you should go to the Scriptorium."

"The Scriptorium?" Nonesuch asked.

From the Latin *scribere*, to write," the bat explained. "The room where books are made. Only Brother Theophilus works there now. He's the next to the last one on the right." Nonesuch looked and saw a monk, taller than most of the others, with red hair poking out of his cowl, who was running his finger over the page of the book before him, an action that made the monks on either side shake their heads in disapproval. "But he'll be here a while yet," the bat continued. "There's a hole under the window by the fifth column on the right-hand side." He nodded down the nave. "That lets you out over the roof of the cloisters at one corner. The Scriptorium is under the diagonal corner." The bat closed his eyes again.

Nonesuch hesitated a moment. Then, while the monks' chanting continued in the choir, he flew where the bat had told him, high in the ceiling, along the white vaulting, down by a red-and-gold window, then through a hole in a broken pane.

The cloister was an open square surrounded by a roofed passage. At the opposite corner was another window that opened into a white-walled room.

The first thing that Nonesuch noticed about the room when he flew through the window was the amount of light; it seemed brighter than the open air. All the windows were of clear glass, and there was a wide skylight in the ceiling. On a table in one corner, well lighted by the skylight and by windows on either side, was a book. Not so big as the great books in the choir: each page was only as long as a man's forearm from elbow to fingertip, and broad in proportion.

It was not a finished book but one in preparation: the pages had not yet been bound together. Each was laid loosely in a leather binder on one side of the desk. A single page, next to the pile on the binder, was still incomplete. On the desk were small pots of paint, mortars for grinding the different colors, pungent oils, and a container with dark brushes. Under the disturbing smell of oil in which the colors were suspended, Nonesuch could tell immediately that one of the pots contained real gold powder.

But the images on the top page in the binder and on the unfinished page drew his attention more closely. The middle part of each page was covered with black letters. In the wide margins around the text were more familiar shapes. A vine started in the lower right-hand corner and spread all around the page, its branches meeting again at the upper left-hand corner. Small tendrils of the vine ran right into the text, marking certain letters with tiny red and gold flowers. Away from the text, the vine became alive with larger flowers in fantastic shapes and colors. Here and there faces peered out of the vine: unicorns, gnomes, mischievous monkeys, solemn toads. From one leaf a tiny bat hung, head down. In the blank spaces away from the vine, bright butterflies fluttered, looking as if in a moment they would fly away from the pages.

Nonesuch had seen all this while hovering above the page. Now he landed on the table, next to the unfinished page. Clouds passed rapidly outside, bringing moving shadows through the window, and the deep-black letters seemed to be moving too. They bent towards each other, as if they were whispering together. Nonesuch became so absorbed in watching these letters that he did not notice that Brother Theophilus, the tall red-haired monk, had returned.

He was carrying an oil lamp, which he carefully hooked on a chain that hung over the centre of the table. In doing so, he leaned over, so that when Nonesuch turned at the shadow that suddenly covered him he found himself hemmed in by the man's body, his wide shoulders and his long black robe. It was impossible to fly up and away!

The small dragon crouched down, looking for a way out, perhaps a spring sideways. His eyes lingered on the page beneath him for a last time; he saw a wise turtle's head that he had not noticed before; it seemed to be winking at him.

"A dragon!" the tall man exclaimed. "A true small dragon!" He stretched out his hand. Nonesuch drew back his head with a warning hiss. The man's hand was long and scholarly; white, except where it was stained with color. Even so, it could easily have crushed the tiny dragon, and the man realized this immediately. He withdrew his hand gently and sat down, gazing at Nonesuch with large, shining eyes.

Then, moving very cautiously, he took up a brush, dipped it in green paint, and sketched a small dragon, less than one-quarter the size of Nonesuch himself, in a space between two vines. Making sure that his movements did not alarm the dragon, he picked up another brush, then another; he tipped in a bluish tint to match the edge of Nonesuch's wings, gold for his eyes, and a hint of red where his belly showed. He laid his brushes down and looked carefully from the dragon to his portrait of him. "It's not so beautiful," he remarked sadly, "but how could it be? I always wanted to see a dragon and now, at last, one has come." He crossed himself, then pushed his chair back from the table. "Go in peace," he told None-such gently, "but come again."

Though he knew there was no danger, Nonesuch thought it proper to leave now. He flew out of the Scriptorium, back through the church, which was empty again, to the column by the choir screen. The bat still hung there, motionless. When Nonesuch landed on the capital above him, the bat spoke without opening his eyes. "Brother Theophilus is a scholar and a scribe. I visit him from time to time. When he prepares his colors, it's my duty to keep insects away." The bat licked his lips thoughtfully. "He acknowledges my function, and even set a bracket in the wall for me to hang on."

"He painted you too," Nonesuch told the bat.

"Did he, now?" After a time the bat remarked, "I hope it doesn't bring me visitors." His legs tensed so that he hung a little higher. "Could you tell if it was me, particularly?"

Nonesuch had never seen a bat so close before; this one looked like any other. "The picture was so small that I really couldn't see," he replied.

The bat relaxed. "Good. I prefer the quiet, anonymous life. You are happier if no one notices you at all. Though it will be good if one of us is in the book."

"He painted me too," Nonesuch admitted.

The bat opened his eyes and looked thoughtfully at the small dragon for some time. "Well, I should imagine so," he replied. "One doesn't see your sort every day. In fact, this is the first time for me as well. Are you very young? You don't seem so."

"I was large and grew smaller," Nonesuch told him.

The bat thought this over. "It was probably a good thing to do," he said at last. "If you were too big to get into our church, you could never see the Apostle window there" – he nodded at the twelve upright glass figures – "or the rose window. There are some carvings behind the choir stalls that are absolutely unique. I'm sure the humans can't see them at all. The carver made them, so he must have wanted someone to see them, perhaps only you and I and the beetles; though naturally we don't all have the same kind of interest in the carvings.''

The bat sighed, as if weary of so much talk, and closed his eyes again. In a moment he began to breathe deeply, fast asleep. Nonesuch flew away from the column and explored the upper reaches of the church. He chose as his own resting-place a capital on which three smiling dragon's heads had been carved. There he had a good view of the two great windows at either end of the nave, as well as of the choir with its stalls and books. From it, he could fly to the Scriptorium without being seen, even when the church was not empty.

He and the bat never had the church to themselves for long. There were services throughout the day and one late at night. For this one, every fourth monk carried in a dim lamp. When the chanting stopped, and a long sermon was being preached, a lantern went here and there among the choir stalls: one of the monks was making certain that none of the others had fallen asleep.

Whenever the bell rang for services, Brother Theophilus joined the other monks. Between times, he returned to his book. Nonesuch often flew out of the church to the Scriptorium as soon as the service ended. He would wait on a deep window ledge until Brother Theophilus sat down; then he flew to a shelf near the monk's table. Finally he perched on an unlit oil lamp that hung directly above the table.

Though the monk never looked up, he knew where Nonesuch was. When the little dragon landed on the lamp, Brother Theophilus would finish whatever he was painting, and then paint another dragon, or, rather, a part of a dragon. He would paint a wing with its individual scalloping, just emerging from behind other figures; a head peeping out of the bushes; or a tail flying away. Soon there was at least one dragon on every page. Only their colors varied. Some were red, some gold, several green, one deep-black with red eyes.

In time, Brother Theophilus began to talk to the little dragon. For a while he seemed to be speaking to himself. Nonesuch had seen his lips moving silently before, when Brother Theophilus thought he was quite alone; and sometimes he might laugh, almost as silently. But now Nonesuch realized that the monk's words were directed at him.

At first Brother Theophilus spoke of the book he was writing and illuminating. It was a "Book of Hours", which contained prayers appropriate for each hour of the day. Though the words on each page were holy, the pictures that accompanied them often had little or nothing to do with these words. Rather, as Brother Theophilus explained, since the words came from God, it was permitted to adorn them with any aspect of His world. Other Books of Hours that have come down to us show a detailed picture of the life of their time. You can find ploughmen and weavers in the pages of such books, woodcutters and stonemasons, splendid knights, bright ladies, ships and soldiers, scenes of battle and scenes of peace.

Thus far, Nonesuch had only seen two pages of Brother Theophilus's book. In the week that had now passed since the dragon's arrival, the monk had finished the page that Nonesuch had first seen and had started on another one. The rest of the pages rested in their loose cover. Whenever he had finished for the day and all the pictures he had painted were quite dry, Brother Theophilus would close this cover, which was of leather, adorned with four blue enamelled crosses, and store the cover and pages in a heavy black box that lay at the back of his work-table. This box had been inlaid with strips of iron by a clever metalworker, so that it seemed encased in an endless net of iron. The heavy lock was inlaid in the wood too. A light chain attached the box to the table. Whenever Brother Theophilus closed the lock on its contents of precious pages, he would remark, as if to himself: "Now my treasure is shut up again." These words made Nonesuch shiver strangely.

In those days, when most books were still made by hand, and when many required years of skilled work, they were rare and costly objects. Noblemen counted their wealth in books owned as well as in land, flocks, manors, and gold. The books Nonesuch had seen in the choir represented part of the abbey's wealth. There were thirty more in the Abbot's library, making this a rich abbey indeed. But the book that Brother Theophilus was making was not for the abbey's use.

When all the pages were completed, when all were bound together inside their cover, this particular Book of Hours was to be an important part of the marriage portion of Lady Blanche, the youngest daughter of Hungerford Castle, by which Nonesuch had been blown before he fetched up against the window of the church of this Abbey of Oddfields.

Once Nonesuch, motionless on his lamp as if he had been an ornament, saw Lady Blanche herself. She was tall, just turned eighteen. Her eyes shone; her cheeks still glowed from the ride to the abbey. She had persuaded the young page who had accompanied her to see to a horseshoe, which might be loose, and talk to the blacksmith's pretty daughter, while she, Lady Blanche, entered the Scriptorium alone.

She was delighted with the progress of her book. As Brother Theophilus turned over the finished pages, she exclaimed over each detail. She was properly impressed by the religious scenes that appeared in the first pages: Christ walking on the waves of the Sea of Galilee, with a bemused seagull perched on his shoulder; Job sitting among the ashes, watched by his three friends, a sad-eyed mouse and two black crickets; Lot's wife just on the point of looking back at the burning Cities of the Plain. But she expressed most enthusiasm at the more recent pages with their animals among the vines. "They might be alive!" she marvelled. "How can you bear to close the pages on them, good brother?"

"Creatures in my book can live without light and air, my lady," Brother Theophilus replied, smiling gently. "They come to life again whenever the pages are opened."

Lady Blanche also smiled. Then she drew in her breath sharply. "There is a dragon hiding here! And here is another!"

"Very small ones, my lady," Brother Theophilus replied. He did not look at Nonesuch. The tiny dragon shivered on his lamp, which swung a little, as if in a breeze.

"Bigger ones would hardly fit on your pages," Lady Blanche commented. "I have often heard of dragons," she added thoughtfully, "but never seen one. Perchance they are all only a dream."

"I hardly think so, my lady."

"In any case, they've kept away from us; as have the wars. Perhaps we should be equally thankful for both." Lady Blanche turned over a couple of loose pages in the cover. On one was a wedding scene, a peasant wedding with the bride and groom marching proudly at the heads of separate processions. She sighed. "*My* bridegroom still has not come. He may be far away on other business."

Lady Blanche's future bridegroom, whom she had only met a few times, was often away on other business. He was Sir Ambrose, the lord of what had once been Grimsby Castle. He was now of sufficient importance in the great world of human affairs to be considered worthy of an alliance with the ancient but almost bankrupt Hungerford Castle. Lady Blanche had been greatly impressed by the stories of his energy and his rapid rise at the royal court. At their brief meetings in the presence of her parents, she had found her suitor curiously distant, though always polite, and so refined that she almost thought it strange he could do so well in this rough world. She had been distressed by the look of pain on her father's face, though she supposed this was because he was soon to lose her, his favorite child. All betrothals must be like this, she thought.

"Other business indeed, my lady," Brother Theophilus replied.

Later that day, when he was alone, except for Nonesuch, who had flown down to the table from his lamp to look more closely at the book, Brother Theophilus began to speak of the nature of dragons. Many considered them completely wicked beasts, he said, but not he. If they were, surely God would not have made them so beautiful. He must have a purpose for them.

In other lands, he said, they were called guardian spirits. They guarded springs, or lakes, or their own treasure. At these words, Nonesuch flew off the table, circled the room, and perched on a high shelf above Brother Theophilus's work-table, twitching his tail from side to side. The monk looked at him keenly. "Is it possible that you understand my words?" he asked. "Can it be that I am not only talking to myself, as I do so often?" He looked long at the little dragon. "Well, I will imagine you can understand me," Brother Theophilus said at last. The bell rang for Vespers. He sighed, closed his book carefully, and locked it in its box.

# CHAPTER VII

## INTO THE BOX

# A

S THE DAYS PASSED, NONE-
SUCH CONTINUED TO WATCH

Brother Theophilus at work. The monk was the only scribe in the abbey at present. In other abbeys, whole groups of writers and illustrators worked busily on sacred manuscripts. Perhaps they knew, or felt, that soon their work would no longer be needed. A few years earlier, Johann Gutenberg had printed his Bible and introduced printing to Europe. In time, books were to become accessible to all, but their loving manufacture by hand would cease.

Brother Theophilus, however, worked on in a tranquil spirit. He was quite satisfied to do his beautiful task as well as he could. He did not mind being alone. ''We are a jealous lot,'' he told Nonesuch. ''Others would certainly comment on my work; they might say that all these dragons have no place in the text among the holy words, but only in the margins where more liberty is permitted.''

While he spoke, Brother Theophilus had been painting yet another dragon. This one was at the top of the page, and to see it more closely without disturbing the painter, Nonesuch left the lamp and flew to the shelf above the side of the table. The new dragon was unlike any that Nonesuch had seen, either in the book or in real life. It had a long, flexible body, a round face with long whiskers, and a look of deep wisdom and benevolence.

"I have seen such a beast in a beautiful scroll that a learned traveller brought from far in the east, from the land of the Emperor of China," Brother Theophilus said. He went on to speak of other Oriental dragons. People in their lands often worshipped them as gods, who brought storms and sunshine, rain and drought. Perhaps, he smiled, they represented the arbitrary powers of nature, signs from the Almighty to humans that they should never take anything for granted.

Suddenly he stopped talking. Footsteps sounded outside the door, and in an instant the Abbot entered. Nonesuch, who had not had time to fly away, remained frozen on his shelf.

"Are you talking to yourself again, Brother Theophilus?" the Abbot asked. "Recently you seem to be doing so more and more." The Abbott bent over the table, as far as his ample belly would permit. "Excellent!" he sighed. "Beautiful! How you praise the Creator's works!" He straightened up. "But what is this?" he cried. "An image of a dragon?" He was looking directly at Nonesuch, who had not stirred a whisker. The Abbot moved as close as he could and leaned forward, pressing his belly against the table. "Of fine jade, with eyes of pure gold!" he exclaimed. "Where could you have found such a statue? I have never seen it before in our Treasury."

"It is not really a holy object, Father Abbot," Brother Theophilus replied.

"True," said the Abbot. "But it is a very beautiful object, wherever it came from."

The bell rang for Lauds then; the two monks departed,

and Nonesuch was able to fly back to the heights of the church, where he reported the Abbot's words to the bat.

"Yes," the bat told him. "The rule of our Order is much less austere than it once was. When St. Benedict founded us, only a few holy objects were permitted. But now we have become much more of the world. Our rooms for noble guests are better-furnished than most of those in the guests' homes. Not all of the statues in these rooms are of saints, by any means. It wasn't surprising if the Abbot, who is a tolerant man, thought Brother Theophilus had a statue of a dragon for his own pleasure. You should see some of the pictures on *his* walls."

The bat, who had spoken while hanging upside down, peered keenly at the vault above him. Three black-beetles were crawling up a curved granite rib in a single file. The bat released his hold, turned in the air, flew up swiftly, and cleaned the beetles off the stone. He returned to his perch and hung there, chewing thoughtfully.

"All the other bats roost in the great cedar of Lebanon in the cloister," he told Nonesuch at length. "They wonder why I choose to stay here in the church. They don't realize how quiet it is, between services, how good and varied is the diet. Air currents and the light of the rose window seem to attract a particularly tasty kind of moth. Then there are the death-watch beetles in the stalls. They'd do even more damage if I weren't here to keep them under control. After all, it's *my* church."

The bat began to talk of the church's history, but had hardly got past its beginnings as a pagan shrine before he fell asleep again, still hanging upside down.

In the next few days Nonesuch, who was by no means content to stay inside the church at all times, learned much more about life in the abbey. He perched in the cloister, watching the monks parade solemnly round and round. From a shelf in the well-stocked pantry, he watched them at meals, at the wooden trestles of the refectory, all eating well and silently, except for the monk assigned each day to read to the others. From high in the air, he saw the monks at work in the wheat and oat fields, finally gathering in the harvest. He saw the work of the bakehouse and the brewhouse, the saddlery and the cobbler's shop.

A few of the monks commented on the strange green bird that had appeared recently. Only old Brother Angelicus, who waved pigeons away from the herb gardens, blinked his milky-blue eyes and remarked, ''We have a dragon among us.'' The other monks smiled kindly at him. Thereafter, even those who had wondered at the shape of the green bird said nothing about it, for fear of being thought as witless as Brother Angelicus.

You may think that such a life would be too quiet, too dull for a dragon, however small. Nonesuch did not find it so. He made himself the protector of the grounds. Several rabbits, who had grown fat on the abbey's excellent green beans, carrots, and celery, found their quiet feeding disturbed by what they took to be an obnoxious insect. Finally they went back to scavenging in the gardens of the peasants, who, however, were much more vigilant than the monks. The Abbot's pet poodle became more sober, kept to the gravel paths, and completely abandoned his favorite game of scratching up the radish beds. Nonesuch even tried to keep the wasps away from the juicy pears, just ripening now on the north wall. There were so many of these determined insects that his raids on them made little difference. Still, the monks remarked to each other that the wasps were especially restive this year, and more apt to take offence.

Nonesuch saw people other than monks on his rounds. In

the past, the abbey had been able to supply all the skilled workers it needed from its own ranks, but no longer. A small group of weavers from a nearby village now furnished them with cloth. A tailor had set up shop almost in the shadow of the walls, for the abbey and its guests, who often needed their clothes mended.

A skilled mason had been employed to repair one of the outer walls of the cloister. With his wife and two sons, he lived in a caravan beside the village inn, a stone's throw from the abbey walls. The mason, known as Supple Will, was also a clever juggler who sometimes performed for the inn's guests. Nonesuch saw him before a small crowd by a bonfire one evening, maintaining an ellipse of three golden rings in the air. The little dragon flew through the smoke, sniffed at one of the rings at the apex of its flight, immediately realized that it was only gilded tin, and flew on to perch on a branch.

"There is a dragon!" a young voice cried. Nonesuch looked down and saw a boy staring up eagerly through the flames.

"Ha! More of your fancies, Simon!" The speaker was a broad young man in red trousers that bulged and shone in the firelight. "Father's foolish tricks must have made your mind wander too." He gestured at the juggler's flying golden rings, then added in a sour voice, "He's more interested in the look of his precious toys than in the money they bring."

"That's likely true, Hubert," the juggler said cheerfully, adding another ring to those in the air and catching yet another on his forehead, where it shone like a diadem. The onlookers applauded and tossed some coins on the ground. The juggler bowed, skilfully kicked the coins up into the air and caught them in his hands without interrupting the flight of the shining rings.

The broad young man sniffed and said, "Maybe you'll ask the dragon to guard your gold, Father."

"I'd be grateful to him, Hubert," the juggler answered mildly, catching his rings one by one and dropping them in his pouch. "Though he wouldn't find it a hard task."

Hubert snorted. "Dragon, indeed! There are no dragons here now that Sir Ambrose is keeping order. They'd be afraid to come."

"He brings monsters of his own," the juggler said, but so low that only Nonesuch heard him.

Although he realized that the juggler was a poor man, Nonesuch felt an unaccountable interest in him and his family. He found a corner of the wall, choked with vines, where he could hide and watch the juggler at work. Supple Will fitted the stones together carefully, breaking off small pieces to fill in the gaps, applying the mortar with patient skill. His young son, Simon, worked with him, seriously learning a mason's craft. Sometimes, as Nonesuch watched them through the vines, he saw the boy's eyes looking in his direction.

Whenever his father could spare him, Simon walked in the cloister. He stared hungrily at the faces and the strange beasts carved on the columns. The boy had found a stone-carver's chisel somewhere, and a crude mallet. He cut away at scraps of stone, forming them into shapes that so far only he understood. His father watched him closely. When Simon carved a sinuous shape just emerging from the stone in each of three squared blocks that were to crown the wall, he remarked, "It seems as if there were dragons rising out of the stone, my son. But if we put them on the wall, they will soon be covered with vines."

"That's how they should be, Father," Simon replied.

The juggler shook his head thoughtfully. The same day, he set the three stones in a row atop the wall. Later, he spoke to one of the stone-cutters who was repairing frost damage to a cornice on the south side of the church. He volunteered to set up scaffolding for him if, at the same time, his younger son could work with him as an apprentice.

Hubert, the older son, sometimes gave his father a hand; but when the work became heavy, he explained that he could not help them further. He always wore his finest clothes, which he should certainly not make dirty with sweat and mortar: he had to make a good impression on prospective employers.

As the bat had remarked, the abbey was by no means separated from the world. It contained several rooms where travelling nobles and wealthy men might stay a night or a week. Hubert thought that one of these should be willing to employ a clever young fellow like himself, who would not scruple to take on any kind of work. He stole his mother's pies to bribe the stewards of passing lords. He opened the gates of peasants' pig-pens so that the lords' soldiers could dine well round their night fires. He always carried a flagon of wine to grease the gullet of any likely serving-man. So far, he had received plenty of praise and encouragement, but nothing more definite.

Then, one day after Hubert watched his father and Simon work on the wall for a full hour, he informed them, smiling in a superior fashion, that he was virtually certain of a position in Sir Ambrose's personal guard. Sir Ambrose himself was now visiting Hungerford Castle on business connected with his betrothal: some minor detail of the contract that needed to be set right. Sir Ambrose was attentive to the smallest detail, Hubert said proudly. More than this, his personal secretary had passed the night only steps away, in one of the guest rooms of Oddfields Abbey. The secretary pretended he had done this to give less trouble at the castle where his lord was lodging; but really, Hubert said with a wink, it was to keep an eye on the surroundings, to learn as much as possible of the sentiment of the local people. Sir Ambrose was well aware that knowledge was power. He had learned that men visiting a monastery spoke even more freely among themselves and to the monks than they would do in a tavern. The secretary, a subtle, smiling man, who turned every word into a joke, knew how to inspire confidences and to collect information that his master might use.

Nonesuch got a good look at Sir Ambrose's secretary when he came, as if by chance, to visit the Scriptorium. He looked at the book that Brother Theophilus was making, the book that one day would become his master's property through Lady Blanche. He spoke pious, appreciative words, all the while stroking his short beard; his eyes shone gaily on the pages as if counting up their worth. Then he went away to leave an offering in the poor-box of the church, leaving behind also a whiff of the perfume with which his beard was scented.

Brother Theophilus had spoken little during his visit; this was quite different from his usual enthusiasm when others came to see his book. He remained silent for a long time afterwards. Then he took up his brushes and drew the figure of a man, a neat, cold figure, richly but quietly dressed, standing in the middle of a small grove of trees. Brother Theophilus spent much time on this figure and on its surroundings. Finally there was, beside the man himself, a number of humble small forest creatures: a squirrel on a branch who seemed to be holding himself especially still lest the man see him. There was also a rabbit trembling beneath a bush; there was an owl in the air, who did not seem to be in flight, as were all the other birds Brother Theophilus had drawn. No, this owl hovered as if frozen in place, as if he were happy to remain forever out of the sight of the quiet, well-dressed man in the centre of the grove: a man who looked round him as though whatever his eye fell on became his: the trees, the grass, the sky—and even the words on the page outside the forest grove. Indeed, the viewer felt that if the quiet man raised his head he would look out of the page, around the room, or through the window into the sky, and possess all of it.

Brother Theophilus looked for a long time at the page he had made. "There are such men," he said at last. Then he took a new brush and touched its tip with green. Working quickly and carefully, he painted a dragon, all green and gold, at the back of the grove. By a trick of perspective, the dragon seemed as large as the quiet man, or much larger. Brother Theophilus touched its scales with red and deepened the gold of its eyes. "Where such men exist," he said, "there must be a dragon too." He stood over his work until all the colors were dry. Nonesuch, who had crouched motionless on his lamp at the approach of Sir Ambrose's secretary, remained still. Finally, Brother Theophilus laid this page on the others in the leather cover, closed the cover, and locked all together in the box at the back of the table.

In the next few days, Nonesuch, unwilling to go far from his book, kept close to the church and the Scriptorium. He had already seen signs of battle in the church, reminders of how humans treated their own kind. Above the great altar and scattered about the columns were statues of a man nailed to a cross. In the chapels were pictures of soldiers thrusting swords into babies and of a man, tied to a tree, being shot full of arrows. There was even a painting of a winged man killing a dragon. It had been a most unfair fight, Nonesuch thought. The dragon was small, no larger than the man; it was probably very young and inexperienced. It was lying on its back while the man thrust his spear through it. Nonesuch decided that he must have surprised the dragon while it was sleeping.

The air in the church hummed with a more exciting kind of combat. The eyes of the Apostles, in their window, seemed to command him to do mighty deeds. The faces of demons carved on some of the columns radiated hatred out into the air; other faces were mild and benevolent, but strong. As Nonesuch flew among these faces, he felt that a battle between them was raging about him. Was this a battle in which he might join?

In the Scriptorium, Brother Theophilus was still touching up his picture of the quiet man in the grove of trees. The Abbot saw him one day and put his broad, fleshy hand on the page. "Who is that man?" he asked. Then he shook his head. "I think I may know. He won't thank you for such a picture, especially with that dragon in the forest measuring him with its eyes."

"There are no more large dragons, Father Abbot," Brother Theophilus said sadly.

"Who can be certain?" the Abbot replied.

When Nonesuch flew back to his own capital in the church again, he found the bat waiting for him. For the first time, the bat seemed excited. "I need you tonight," he told Nonesuch.

It concerned the new carvings, portraying the raising of Lazarus from the dead, that had been added to the north outer wall of the choir. The bat loved this subject, and would hang for hours from the choir screen to watch the carver at work. He was a timid Flemish artist who spoke neither English nor Latin. He had worked almost in complete silence; sometimes he would sing to himself in his own language, in a low, sweet voice. The carvings were done now. Soon they were to be painted in bright colors, all but the wood-colored body of Lazarus, which was to be covered with a clear lacquer. The bat had learned this from the conversation of the monks, who did not approve of unpainted holy objects. But the wood would not be dry enough to paint for a month; meanwhile, the carver was working elsewhere.

The fresh surface of the wood, the bat said, would certainly attract boring beetles. He had been able to take care of these by himself, thus far. But a greater danger threatened the carvings. The other bats had told him of a half-wild cat in the forest that would even climb their own cedar to hunt them. It used to sharpen its claws on tree bark; by chance, its favorite elm tree had been cut down for these new carvings, and it wanted revenge. It had already scratched savagely at the Flemish carver as he walked quietly around the abbey walls. The cat had entered the church while he worked and watched the carving from behind the altar with a sly, malign expression. "He will attack the finished carvings themselves," the bat whispered.

The bat wouldn't think of interfering with such a creature. "He'd crunch me like lettuce," he told Nonesuch. "But you'd make him think twice, small as you are. I think he'll come tonight, very late."

This was indeed proper work for a dragon! The bat's words made Nonesuch forget all his other thoughts of the secret battles within the church. So it was that, long past midnight, when a glorious moon painted the stones with soft colors and tall shadows, Nonesuch sat, very still, at the foot of a statue of a sorrowful king with a curly beard, in a niche in the wall facing the carvings outside the choir, listening for the pat-pat and whisper of the cat's paws.

But it was human feet that sounded near by: heavy footsteps. A bulky body deposited itself on the altar steps, then a lighter one passed by to the foot of the nearest choir seats and sat down too. There was a smell of sweat, of rose-water, and of smoke. Nonesuch recognized Hubert, the juggler's son, and Greasy Clement, a tiny, ignorant man who did the jobs no one else wanted. Greasy Clement cleaned out the kitchen ovens, the spit, and the cauldrons, and his face and clothes were always covered with grease from his mean tasks. Of all the monks, only the Abbot and Brother Theophilus would talk to him. Brother Theophilus let Greasy Clement watch him at work, as long as he kept well away from all the pages. Clement's voice now showed that he was delighted that a person with as much presence and apparent importance as Hubert would actually want his company.

Now he waited for the larger man to speak. Only after a long time, in which Hubert's hoarse breathing showed that he was too full of sorrow for words, did Clement venture timidly, ''Imagine him treating you that way!''

Hubert remained silent. He was remembering again how Sir Ambrose's secretary had let his eyes stray over him thoughtfully, taking in his red trousers — which were, in fact, the very reddest he owned, put on just for this interview — and remarking in a regretful tone but with twinkling eyes, ''Alas, my good man, we could never find a uniform to suit you. You would not be comfortable.''

''Anything would do for me, my lord,'' Hubert had mumbled. He writhed as he thought of it now. He could almost hear his own voice saying these words again.

The secretary had raised his eyebrows. ''But 'anything' will not do for Sir Ambrose. He is most particular that those who are around him should be happy and well at ease. Those who are not happy — for example, those who bulge out of their uniforms — are of no use to him.'' And the secretary had continued to smile until Hubert found he could do nothing but back away.

He did not know, of course, that the secretary had never once thought of him as a possible recruit for Sir Ambrose's personal guard: a single glance had made that idea ridiculous. Instead, the secretary had for a time considered Hubert for the job of tax-collector. Sir Ambrose had adopted the practice of employing collectors who were strangers to their district and who made this unpopular profession still more so by their gross manners. His most useful collectors would take the peasants' cows, grain, and pigs, trample through their huts, slit their straw mattresses, and laugh as if it were all a great joke. Such treatment loosened people's tongues. It was a good device to learn which ones were disaffected, so that later Sir Ambrose's men could deal suitably with them. But after talking to Hubert and watching him when he was not aware of it, the secretary had decided he would not be capable even of this occupation: he was just the kind of man, the secretary thought, whom the peasants would delight in outwitting, let him bluster as he would.

All these points of higher policy had been lost on Hubert. "I wronged myself by aiming too low," he declared at last. "I should have spoken to the master himself, not one of his minions. I know where Sir Ambrose passes on his way to church. I will stand where I can speak to him; where he cannot avoid speaking to me."

Greasy Clement cleared his throat quietly. "They say that Sir Ambrose puts complete trust in his secretary. Even if you could find a post with Sir Ambrose, you would not wish to have an enemy even closer to him."

"Once I was with Sir Ambrose, I would need fear no enemy," Hubert declared. Then, after a time: "Still, he is a malicious man, that secretary. One can see it in his eyes."

Both men sat quiet. Greasy Clement spoke timidly. "There is work here, at the abbey, which avoids all malice." He handed Hubert an apple from beneath his cloak.

"Work here!" Hubert cried. He looked down at the apple

and flung it from him. It bumped along the floor to the centre of the choir. "To watch all the fat monks, who live as if they were lords themselves!"

"Some make beautiful things," Greasy Clement offered.

"Do you mean the one with the book?" Hubert demanded.

"It is a beautiful book; it has all the world in it."

"It is a wicked book, from what I hear," Hubert declared. "They say it has dragons in it."

"What is that sound?" Greasy Clement's voice was fearful. "I heard a hiss, and the beating of wings!"

"You are a craven!" Then Hubert snickered. "Perhaps it was a dragon itself; one of those great wicked beasts. I never could stand the thought of them. It's lucky indeed that none could come into this holy place."

Nonesuch settled down again, crouching tensely at the foot of the sorrowful king.

Greasy Clement did not venture to contradict Hubert's judgement of dragons. After a time, the fat man continued: "But there are other things in that book, I'll wager. He paints with gold, does he not?" He waited, staring before him, until the small man shook his head and grunted in agreement.

"There *is* true gold on his pages," he admitted.

"True gold, *you* say!" Hubert retorted. "Who knows how much of it is true gold? Gold can be mixed with other things; I know this for a fact. Do you think my father's toys are gold, though they shine so? No a whit of it!"

"But Brother Theophilus does get gold for his book," Greasy Clement objected. "I heard the treasurer and Brother Aureus, the gold-beater, talk of it once."

"Ah," said Hubert, "he got it indeed, but did he use it? Of all the gold that was given him, how much is really in the pages of his wicked book? There must be sheets of gold still, between the pages, or stored in that box. Indeed, who knows what else is in the box? Who keeps order in this place? That wicked man, with his paints and brushes, and his dragons, can wander where he will. All but I are too innocent to suspect his real purpose! Did you not tell me that jewels were missing from the Treasury?''

''They were only mislaid; they were found since.''

''Who knows how many were lost and how many returned?'' Hubert retorted. ''The rest of them must be in that box, too.'' Then Hubert looked at Greasy Clement, who was nodding his head in wonder. No one had ever said so many words to him in his life. ''In that box,'' Hubert repeated.

Nonesuch waited to hear no more. He had felt the hunger in the fat man's voice as he spoke of the book and the box and the riches he supposed they contained. It was a growing hunger, not to be withstood. Very soon, he knew, the man would rise and make his way to the Scriptorium.

The bells rang for Matins, the darkest hours before dawn. Greasy Clement slid away without a sound before the monks could enter the church. Hubert rose, too, ran stooping to the wall, and slouched along it towards the back of the church as the file of monks with their torches entered. One of them stooped to pick up the apple from the floor. Nonesuch flew up, the shortest way, taking no care to hide himself in flight. He heard gasps below him, and an old voice that cried, ''A dragon! I have seen it!'' But he did not pause. Out the hole in the window he flew, out over the cloister and through the window of the Scriptorium.

Brother Theophilus was in the room. He had worked late the day before and had left a page to dry when he was called away by the bell for Vespers. Now, on the way to Matins, he had stopped to look at the book again. He was halfway between the wall table and the door, his back turned to the table. The last page was dry, glowing in the fresh young moonlight. On this page Nonesuch landed, ready to defend it with his life when Hubert entered.

But it should not come to that, he thought. When, instead of sheets of gold in the book and jewels in the box, Hubert found a real dragon, even the smallest one, how he would run! How he would howl! Nonesuch ruffled his wings and stretched his claws, ready for his enemy.

But Brother Theophilus had turned back from the door, his face troubled. Two monks passed the door on the way to the church; they looked at him in surprise. The bells rang again. Brother Theophilus looked at his book. In the moonlight, he did not notice Nonesuch, who, indeed, was almost the size of the dragon painted on the page, the dragon watching a quiet man in a grove of trees. The monk walked to the book and shut it firmly. He slid it into the box and turned the key in the lock. Then, his face still troubled, he followed the other monks into the church.

As Brother Theophilus's shadow passed out of the Scriptorium, Hubert entered it. He didn't hesitate. He picked up the box, then realized it was chained to the table. But the staple that held the chain to the box was weak. Hubert sat on the table and pulled the chain free from the box with a frantic jerk. He spent a minute trying to hide the box under his shirt. Finally, he took it openly in his arms and ran out the door, along one side of the empty cloister, and out through a crack in the broken wall. No one saw him go.

# CHAPTER VIII

# THE LONG SLEEP

# THE THEFT WAS NOT DIS-COVERED UNTIL THE NEXT

morning, when Brother Theophilus returned to the Scriptorium. His cry of woe woke the bats in their cedar of Lebanon. They fluttered up, blackening the sky around its green branches. The monks who heard him turned here and there, distracted, sharing his loss before they knew what it was. No one but Greasy Clement suspected that Hubert was the thief; and he did not dare to speak. All kinds of folk passed in and out of the abbey. The monks, who had laughed at Hubert's size and his red trousers, could hardly imagine that he would have enough enterprise to steal anything.

Messengers were sent out to search for the thief, in vain. Hubert hid in the forest by day and travelled at night. Whenever he rested, he tried to pick the lock; but this was far beyond his skill. He had no tools with which to break the box open. He ate nothing during his flight, so that by the time he entered London he was able to slip the box under his waistband.

At last Hubert was sure that no one would recognize him. He sat in the corner of a low tavern in Cheapside with the box resting on the bench beside him. A small, pock-marked man, dressed as a respectable artisan, approached in a friendly manner, not appearing to notice how fearfully Hubert clutched the box beneath his elbow. The pock-marked man hailed Hubert as a stranger, a traveller from the great world outside. He was sure, he said, that Hubert had news to tell of these troubled times. But, first, he must drink a mug of ale to ease his throat.

Then, very courteously, the pock-marked man listened to Hubert's stories of life at Sir Ambrose's court and of his own importance there. With each new, imaginary step in Hubert's advancement his new friend insisted on treating him to another mug of ale. ''I can see they know how to appreciate merit out there,'' he said. ''You'll find it the same here, in London: you'll go very far. Drink up, now.''

So it was that in a short time, when Hubert was sound asleep, his friend was able to ease the box from under his arm. Two hours later Hubert awoke with a desolate cry. Amid the laughter of the tavern he ran off, bulging and bumping through the dirty alleys of London, where his fate need concern us no longer.

The new thief did not carry the box far, just to the low window of a cellar in a nearby mews. He knew how to ease the window catch and slip into the cellar. There he deposited the box carefully between some old pieces of timber near a pile of coal. He had decided to leave the box in here, his favorite hiding-place, while he tended to other urgent business.

His business involved a bolt of fine satin in a draper's shop, a shop that seemed to be poorly guarded by its sleepy owner. The thief had not suspected how quickly the owner would wake up when there was any danger to his goods. The crowd in the street eagerly joined in the chase. The thief was caught and, after proper legal formalities, hanged.

No one came for the box in the cellar; it stayed there a very long time.

Nonesuch had not submitted tamely to being shut up. But though the pages of the book were too loose to crush him, he was so pressed between them that he could hardly move. The box was closed and locked, and he was in the dark. He struggled furiously and wiggled to the edge of the page. Even in his haste and anger he kept his claws in, for fear of tearing the fine vellum. Still, he moved forward until his nose bumped against one of the iron strips that bound the box together.

He was turned in all directions as Hubert shifted the box in his arms. Nonesuch could hear the fat man's fearful panting and the beat of his heart. Through cracks in the box he could smell Hubert's sweat, which by now was making the box slippery to hold. Once Hubert let it fall, which loosened the book's cover and jarred Nonesuch down to the bottom. When he recovered they were once more on the way. He was jammed against the wood of the box, this time at a spot that was not crossed by an iron strip. He began to bite at the wood to make his way out.

But the wood, seasoned oak, was very tough. His jaws were made for slashing and devouring, not for gnawing. As time passed, it seemed that he was making no progress at all. Or perhaps this was because he was growing very sleepy.

It was the effect of his own breath in this enclosed space. Many old stories tell us that the breath of dragons was poisonous, or at least that it could make humans become very drowsy. Whatever the truth of such tales, Nonesuch found his eyes always closing. The box was quite still now. He slept deeply; for a time his dreams were more vivid than the thoughts of his waking life.

Dragons' dreams are far-ranging: some ancients thought that the whole world may be contained in such dreams. The lives of the people with whom Nonesuch had been concerned passed through his sleep in bright images.

Hubert had boasted to his family of his hope of a position with Sir Ambrose but naturally had said nothing of his treatment by the secretary. The family agreed, each keeping his doubts to himself, that Hubert had got the post, and had so gone up in the world that he would no longer associate with them.

The juggler and his younger son continued to work at the abbey, where some wall or pavement was always in need of repair. In time Simon became a stone-carver himself, whose skill took him around the countryside. Whenever possible he would embellish his work: a portal, a window, or a capital with the head or whole body of a small dragon. He liked to work in high places. Two hundred years later, at the time of the Puritan revolution, all of his work escaped the destruction by the religious reformers' hammers and long poles. If you visit these churches today, you can still see the dragons, smiling down on headless saints and apostles without hands.

Though Sir Ambrose certainly didn't show it, he was more pleased than otherwise at the theft of the book. He took its loss as a reason to break off his proposed match with Lady Blanche. He had already found a richer alliance; if the bride was dull and coarse-featured, what of that? He need not see much of her. He would have dropped the connection with Hungerford Castle in any case. But this loss of the book, an important part of the marriage settlement, gave him a convenient excuse. Because of it, he did not have the thief pursued as vigorously as he would otherwise have done.

Lady Blanche grieved for a time, as was only proper. But she soon realized that she was mourning more for the book than for her bridegroom. Being a sensible girl, she hinted to her relieved parents that she was not quite ready to retire from the world. After a suitable time she was married to a scholarly, absent-minded knight, with whom she got on very well.

The loss of the book struck Brother Theophilus hardest of all. ''I had come to love the little dragon too well,'' he said to himself, ''so that it flew away. Even the book was taken from me.'' In time, he made other books, though none as beautiful as this one; he never painted another dragon.

Nonesuch woke from a dream in which Brother Theophilus was gazing at him sadly and thought sleepily that he really should look at the world outside the box. He began to bite at the wood again, but fell asleep before he had broken off more than a few splinters. After a time, he woke and nibbled at the wood again; but he grew bored and began to look about him, using the light of his own eyes.

He was lying between two pages. By arching his back, he could spread the pages and look down on the one beneath him, which happened to be the one he had seen on his first visit to the Scriptorium. There were the vines and the flowers, and the small animals Brother Theophilus had drawn, all surrounding the thick black letters that lay there quietly as if they too were sleeping. Nonesuch decided to follow the path of a vine all around the page, and he crept along, from letter to letter, until the vine seemed to be a path through a black forest. He crawled up one side of the page, across, and down the other side. He looked across at the words as he went by; soon they seemed to be chuckling at him, daring him to find out their secret. He could almost hear them say, ''We are all here, waiting for you.''

And, in time, he slept again. When he awoke (and he realized that this was long afterwards), he began to explore the book again, crawling between other pages that he had never seen before.

Now that he had all the time in the world, and more, to examine the book, he found new wonders everywhere in it, and many familiar things that made him remember his days in the Abbey of Oddfields.

In the margins of such books, scribes often drew pictures that they would not dare put among the holy words in the main parts of the pages. Nonesuch saw the abbey again, from the east, as he had first approached it. He also saw it from the south side, where the wall was broken to show the ''Necessarium'', as the common lavatory was called. Just emerging from the yellow-and-green doors of this building was the Abbot: fat, sly, loose-jowled, kindly, in the act of knotting his robe about him. In another margin, Nonesuch found an old monk whose task it was to watch the corn, but who always fell asleep in the sun; the crows used to take turns fanning his face gently, Nonesuch remembered, so that he would go on sleeping. There was a crow by him in the margin now, keeping him asleep forever.

There were other monks as well: pious Brother Catechismus, who sold some of the poultry from the kitchen and kept the money for himself. Brother Theophilus had caught him in the very act of handing over a goose with one hand and accepting some coins with the other from the owner of the castle inn. Brother Catechismus's robe was spread wide so that no one could see him. But very little had been missed by Brother Theophilus's mild, bright eyes.

As time passed, Nonesuch must have crawled through every page of the book; but he always seemed to find something new.

And often he slept. He was not hungry at all. Only sometimes, when pale earwigs squeezed through cracks in the box, he took care of them. He had all he wanted to eat. But he was growing still smaller. He realized this once when he came to a large golden ''T'' at the beginning of a chapter. When he had passed it before, his body just fit nicely over the top of the letter, from end to end. Now large bars of it extended past his nose and past his tail. His left wing, which before had easily covered the upright part of the ''T'', now scarcely reached two-thirds of the way down. Really, Nonesuch thought, he should eat more or he would shrink away to nothing. But he forgot this danger and slept again; he dreamed that his grandmother was singing to him in her cracked, vibrant voice, as she had when he was very young.

Sometimes, because there was, after all, a world outside the box – though he thought of it less and less often – Nonesuch bit at the wood again. His gnawing must have attracted some wood-boring beetles from the outside, because once, when he bit at the box, half asleep, the wood broke suddenly and a dim, dirty light shone through. Then it was easy to enlarge the hole; once he had begun, he didn't want to stop. In a short time, no more than a month, in fact, he was able to stick his head out of the box and squeeze his body through the hole.

It hardly seemed worth while coming out. He was in a cellar full of junk. Above him was a patchy framework of loose beams and broken sticks, laced with cobwebs. Scraps of cloth hung here and there, pieces of broken chairs, fragments of crockery; a stained straw mattress swarming with straw-colored bugs lay against a beam. At one side, beneath black wooden stairs, was a small coal heap, up and down which black-beetles were marching in two orderly lines.

Nonesuch flew up — almost surprised that he still remembered how to fly. The light, such as it was, came from a shuttered window. Nonesuch peeked between the shutter's doors and saw the glass, thick with dust and sealed shut. Through it he could see another trash heap in an alley outside. No one passed by.

He flew back to his book, and just in time. A venturesome cockroach had stuck his head into the hole in the box. He scuttled away — fortunately for him, *out* of the box — as Nonesuch approached. The dragon crawled back into his box, and sniffed round it carefully to be sure that no other insect had entered. But he realized that the hole left the box open to any passing insect. He crawled out of the box, and looked round the cellar floor until he found a wooden peg whose broad end just closed the hole. He took it in his jaws by the thin end and backed into the box, plugging the hole after he had entered.

He returned to his book; but soon he realized that a larger animal was roaming among the cellar beams. He could hear its feet patter and the thumps as it leapt from one level to another. Thus far, it had kept away from his box.

Sometimes Nonesuch slept again, but his sleep was light and his dreams were troubled. He saw an angel with a proud, stern face, like one he had seen in the church, flying around the city streets among great crowds of people, striking them with a black rod. The rod left black marks wherever it touched them and the people fell to the ground and lay still. Men were gathering up the bodies. The faces of the bearers were covered with masks; some had long beaks on them, like birds. Others chewed herbs, or burnt pungent herbs in small vessels so that the smoke covered their faces. They were piling the bodies into carts and hauling them away to deep pits, which were almost full but still had enough room, it seemed, to contain all the bodies in the world. Nonesuch awoke and looked at the figures on the pages of his book, which seemed to be living peacefully without any such dreams. He heard the sound of a leap outside: a substantial body landed on one of the beams. Nonesuch pushed out the plug of wood and squeezed out of the box.

On a slanting beam was the longest rat he had ever seen. The rat's patchy black body was more than a foot long and his tail, which hung down out of sight, longer than that. He had a thin neck and a narrow, bald head. As Nonesuch approached, the rat turned his head to look at him with an expression of mild surprise.

# CHAPTER IX

# THE RAT'S STORY

# THE RAT TURNED HIS BODY TO FACE NONESUCH

squarely. The dragon flew to a higher beam, in case the animal had any idea of attacking him. The last time he had faced a rat, he had been much larger. It had been long since he had fought anything at all; so long that the very idea of fighting had grown strange to him. Still, he would not flee. It might be foolhardy, or even stupid, to stand up to an animal as large as this, but he could not think of abandoning his box and its contents.

As the rat continued to watch him, swaying his long neck to and fro, Nonesuch rose on his claws and curved his wings forward. If he attacked, he thought, he should launch himself at a spot on the rat's spine, too far back for the animal's teeth to reach him. The rat was not so securely perched on his beam: if he turned quickly on it, he might fall off.

But the rat showed no desire for battle. His eyes remained mild and inquisitive. Clearly he thought Nonesuch was some kind of insect. But rats ate insects. Well, Nonesuch thought, when he had seen how this particular insect could sting, he would leave it well enough alone. The rat only continued to look at him curiously, as if he could not believe what he saw.

''Who are you?'' he asked finally.

"A dragon," Nonesuch replied.

The rat seemed to be making an effort not to laugh. "Apart from your size," he replied at last, "which makes the whole idea ridiculous, your shape isn't quite right."

"What did you say?" Nonesuch demanded. He curved his wings and bristled his neck scales.

The rat looked at him even more closely. "At least," he said in a courteous voice, "you are different from any of the dragons I have seen."

"You saw a dragon!" Nonesuch exclaimed. "Where?"

The rat gestured with his long nose towards a very messy pile of paper in one corner. "Over there some place."

"Where is he now?" Nonesuch demanded.

The rat considered the tone of the question. "Not a living one, of course," he explained. "He'd hardly fit into the cellar, would he? There's a picture of one in that pile. I'll find it for you presently."

He looked at Nonesuch again, at some length, and cleared his throat. "I must admit," he told the dragon in a more respectful tone, "that I've never seen anything like you, whatever you are. You kept yourself well hidden."

"I had no reason to come out before." For the moment, Nonesuch had decided not to tell the rat about his box, much less about the book it contained.

The rat nodded wisely. "You have even less reason to come out now," he declared. "This cellar is no better than a dank and foul prison."

Nonesuch looked around again. The cellar was certainly untidy, but also quiet and sheltered. "It doesn't seem as bad as that," he remarked. "Still, if you don't like it, why don't you go outside?"

The rat looked startled at the suggestion. "Oh no," he

whispered, "I never go out! Death is out there! They all fall in the street, my people as well as the humans. From the upper windows I can see carts coming to carry them away. But there is no need to go outside to learn what is happening in the world. I'll show you," he added. "Just let me fetch the dragon I was mentioning."

While the surprised Nonesuch watched him, he leaped from his beam, disappeared behind the mattress, and soon returned dragging a large sheet of paper. He bit a hole near one edge of it and, stretching up against a beam, hung it from a nail.

The paper was covered with letters, except for a picture in the upper left quarter. Nonesuch looked at the sheet for a long time. This, his first sight of a printed page, did not attract him. The coarse and runny letters that covered the paper left no room for a proper margin, and had clearly been put on without love or skill. Furthermore, he wondered who could have had the audacity to paint such a picture as the one he saw. It showed a man standing on a rock in the middle of a river, dressed in armor unlike any Nonesuch had seen before. Sharp, curved blades were attached to the outside of the armor, projecting at all angles. In the water was a large, clumsy, crudely drawn dragon, who was just crawling onto the rock. The knight held out his sword stiffly and smiled at the dragon in a superior fashion.

"That was a notable encounter," the rat informed Nonesuch. "It was the Dragon of Wantly Fell: a beast of great terror; whenever it was cut, its wounds healed of themselves. But the noble knight covered himself with this wonderful armor. When the Dragon seized him, the blades cut its body into pieces, which fell into the river and were washed away before they could join together again."

The rat looked at Nonesuch, waiting for him to be properly impressed. He started back when the little dragon said, ''I don't believe it.''

''You don't believe what?''

''Any of it. Dragons don't heal by themselves. But, even more, no dragon would be so stupid.''

''No, no,'' the rat replied quickly. ''The dragon wasn't stupid; but the knight was too clever for him. You can see how the blades covered his armor. It took all the armorers in Sheffield a week and a day, working together by candlelight, to make that armor.''

''It might have taken them a year and a day,'' Nonesuch retorted. ''But why would the dragon throw himself on the blades?''

''Why, to devour the knight,'' the rat told him. ''Wouldn't you have done that – that is, if you were somewhat bigger?''

''If I *had* wanted to eat the knight, which I wouldn't have done, even when I was as large as the animal in the picture – and, in point of fact, I was once a good deal larger – I would have seized that log on the cleft in the rock with my tail and pounded him a bit until the armor was loose enough to come off easily. *Then*, I suppose, I would have eaten him, if I had the least desire to do such a thing. In my day, we had learned to leave humans alone. Your Dragon of Wantly must have come from a degenerate family. I'm surprised he lasted as long as he did, even if he was able to heal his own wounds, which I don't believe. Did all this happen very long ago?''

''Oh, no,'' the rat told him. ''It says, 'The wicked beast of Wantly Fell, not twenty years ago. The terror of all that did there dwell, in truth I tell you so.' ''

Nonesuch looked at the picture for another minute before answering. ''Well, the people of Wantly Fell, wherever that is, couldn't have been very intelligent either. I suppose they and the dragon deserved each other. In my time, I'm sorry to say, people knew of ways to deal with dragons besides single combat. Where in the world did you learn all this?''

The rat seemed surprised at the question. ''Why, I read it,'' he replied. ''It says so there.'' He pointed with his nose at the hanging sheet of paper.

Nonesuch stared at him.

''The cellar is full of books,'' the rat explained. ''I know a great deal, more than any other rat, I think; and it all comes from books and from broadsheets, like this one about the Dragon of Wantly Fell. You may not believe it, but it's all written down, so it must be true.''

Nonesuch reserved his judgement on this last sentence. The fact that the rat knew how to read interested him much more than the truth and falsehood of what was written. And the rat, who was not a little proud of his knowledge, was glad to tell him how he had come by it.

A family of weavers had once occupied the house, the rat told Nonesuch. They were busy, practical, prosperous people who made good cloth and sold it at good prices. They had broad, tidy showrooms upstairs. Only, they threw all their waste material down the cellar and never cleaned it out, leaving room only for the coal-pile. This had gone on for generations. ''A rat knows what goes on under the surface of things,'' he said proudly. They had all packed suddenly and gone away now, he added; he didn't know where. Surely they would return soon.

All this family had looked down on the old grandfather, who had once been a skilled weaver, but whose hands had grown too stiff for any real work. The tall, mild, white-haired old man kept to himself and took his simple meals alone in his room, in which he had many books: mostly the so-called chap-books sold for a penny or so by peddlers. He read these for company, and taught the children to read as well, until such time as they took on their elders' attitude and became ashamed to visit him.

The rat had often watched the old man and his books through a hole in the plaster of the wall of his attic room. He explained to Nonesuch that the walls had many tunnels and passages, through which he could readily crawl. He could watch the family's activities without being seen; which was just as well, since they would have smoked him out or sent a ferret after him. Only the grandfather saw his bright eyes in a crack in the wall one day; but he told none of the others. Instead, he left out scraps of bread and cheese from his own supper and shut out the family cat.

In return, the rat kept the old man's room clear of earwigs and cockroaches, who would have nibbled at the chap-book pages. Then, when the grandfather taught the children to read, taught them how letters were put together to make sounds, the rat watched from his crack in the wall. Sometimes, indeed, he imagined that the grandfather placed his lesson books so that he, the rat, could see them. Because he was a curious but patient animal, he had learned to read much more quickly than the children. He believed the grandfather knew how much he had learned. During the last few months of his life, the old man would often read aloud from his chap-books. These stories, the Fables of Aesop, were the ones the rat still loved best. He told Nonesuch the story of the fox and the crow, and of the frogs who chose a king.

After the old man's death, the family tossed his chap-books down into the cellar. The rat had been reading them ever since. Now he was the proud guardian of his own library;

he knew many stories he could not have learned otherwise.

In the following days, the rat was very eager to share with Nonesuch the stories he had read. He told him of a knight who travelled in magic lands, performed marvellous deeds, and married the emperor's daughter, and other stories of brave knights who rescued beautiful maidens and helped the poor. The dragon thought of the knights he had seen, who had certainly helped no one but themselves. "If you could only read," the rat said, "you could learn many such stories by yourself."

"If I could read, I could choose any book I wanted," Nonesuch replied. "I'd prefer that. Why shouldn't I read?"

"Why not, indeed?" the rat said. "I'll teach you."

This took only a few days. It might seem an unbelievably short time; but you should remember that many animals must learn things much faster than humans can. The rat, at the age of seven, was already full-grown, even past his prime. And Nonesuch, in the present year, 1665, was over two hundred and fifty years old. He was already full of his grandmother's wise sayings and more experience of the world than any human could possess. Besides this, he had been sleeping for two centuries inside a book that had contained all the learning and love of Brother Theophilus and other good and wise men. So that, once the rat had told him the names and sounds of the different letters and showed him how they were put together, he began to read as if he had always known how. It disturbed him that the spelling of words was sometimes irrational – as English spelling was, and still is – but he accepted this as the sort of thing to be expected from a human invention.

Of course, he tried to read his own book inside the box. At first he was almost afraid to look at it, lest its stories turn out to be as frivolous and unlikely as those of the chap-books. But he soon realized, almost with relief, that though he liked the sounds of the words, he could not understand them. The words were Latin, a language he did not know. Though many of the monks in the abbey had spoken to each other in Latin, Brother Theophilus had used English in Nonesuch's presence, probably realizing that he was an English dragon.

He was happy to note that the people, and the animals, in his book were much more beautiful than those in any of the books or broadsheets in the cellar. The dragons seemed especially beautiful. None of them, he was sure, would act in a way that would bring discredit to his race.

One evening the rat came to him and whispered, in great excitement, that he had been listening to the birds on the rooftops. A rumor was going round that far to the north, in Sherwood Forest, where the famous outlaw Robin Hood had once ruled, the situation was again as it had been before man ever came there. There were no traps, no ferrets or dogs, no plagues or wars, only a few friendly, harmless forest creatures. Many of the birds were flying there.

"I have been thinking of going to find such a place myself," the rat told him. "Indeed, I will go: its pull is so strong that I can stay here no longer. More than likely I will die on the way. But you could come with me. It would be company for both of us, and you could look out for danger better than I. And drive it away, too, if it came near. One day we could live peacefully in the beautiful forest and never see the inside of a cellar again."

Nonesuch looked around him at the dead, dusty cellar. Even at this great distance, it seemed that he could smell the clean woodland breezes. He flew up to the window and looked at the empty street outside. He let his eyes sweep the cellar floor. They came to his box and stopped there. Voices seemed to be calling to him: voices of the words inside the pages — though he still did not understand these words. There were smaller, clearer voices, which must be the little dragons painted in the book, calling to him too.

"I can't go," he told the rat sadly. "I must stay here with my treasure."

"Your treasure?" The rat seemed puzzled, then he nodded his head. "Of course, all dragons have treasures; I read it somewhere. So the books were right about that, at least."

"My treasure is different," Nonesuch told him.

"It must be," the rat agreed. "You yourself are hardly a usual dragon."

Still, he said, he would make the trip to the north, to the great forest. His eyes shone. "I have read about so many adventures that now it is time for me to undertake one of my own. Since you will be here in the cellar, I will often think of it. Otherwise, I would be glad to forget it, books and all."

Nonesuch had gone back inside his box when the rat left the cellar for the last time.

# CHAPTER X

# A FIERY DRAGON

# THE FAMILY OF WEAVERS NEVER RETURNED TO THE

house. What Nonesuch had dreamt and the rat had seen from the window was the great plague, the "black death", which had killed more than one-quarter of the population of Europe three centuries before. It had struck again and again since, and was now making its last appearance in the streets of London. For safety, the weavers had decided to leave the city for the north, near Barnet, where they owned a small shepherd's hut, and wait out the plague there. Many Londoners were leaving the city at this time, often carrying the plague with them. All the members of the family died of it in the isolated hut where they had hoped to find safety.

Nonesuch slept; the years slipped by. The plague came to an end; the great city licked its wounds and buried its dead. Many Londoners regarded the Great Fire that destroyed so much of the city in the next year, 1666, as a final cleansing. The fire narrowly missed the weavers' house — very narrowly indeed: the house was right in its path but, unaccountably, the flames swerved aside just before they reached it. A second cousin of the head weaver took possession of the house but, fearing it might still contain the miasmas of the plague, refused to live in it. For the next hundred years the house was leased as a low hotel, then as a tavern, then as a warehouse for a firm of ironmongers. None of the tenants bothered to clean up the cellar properly.

In the eighteenth century, a gentleman with a spacious house in a more fashionable part of London and an estate in Scotland bought the house to use the old showroom as a laboratory for studying the new science of chemistry. His prudent steward gave the cellar a good cleaning, burning most of the trash. He brought up Nonesuch's box, which he took for a black block of wood, to serve as a support for laboratory apparatus.

Nonesuch awoke from a dream of a fiery lake to the sound of human voices. The accents were quite new to him. Even from within his box the air smelled different than it had when he had last been awake: no longer moldy and dusty, but sharp and disturbing. There was a bubbling sound, too, which he could not identify.

A door opened and shut as the humans left the room. After a time, Nonesuch began to push out the plug of wood from his box. A new coating of paint, which had been laid on two months before, had sealed it shut. He had to grab one end of the plug in his teeth and jiggle it back and forth before it was loose enough to be forced out.

As he squeezed out of his hole, Nonesuch was surrounded by a draft of hot air. His box lay on a wide table beside an iron brazier full of burning charcoal. A metal rod rose from the box to support a fat polished-brass vessel with a curved, tapering neck that sat in the centre of the charcoal.

Nonesuch flew up, away from the heat, and circled the contraption curiously. But someone might come in at any moment. He dropped to the table-top again. Further down the table was another brazier with another bubbling flask. A second table was covered with brown and green bottles, boxes, piles of paper, and two upright charts with strange symbols. On one wall was a large picture of a golden dragon swallowing its own tail. From holes in the dragon's breast, drops of black blood fell into the foreground of the picture.

Before Nonesuch could examine this picture more closely, the door opened and a beam of light swung over the table. He flattened himself on its surface. A sandy-haired man in a brown coat, with a tartan neckerchief above his collar, entered the room clutching a full pile of books in his arm. These blocked his vision, so that even when he turned he would not be able to see the little dragon. Nonesuch realized this immediately; he flew low over the table towards a fireplace with a bright coal fire, and hid behind a massive fire-iron shaped like a grinning dog.

The man ranged the books on a shelf, grumbling to himself as he looked at each title. ''Mair o' his lairdship's folly! *The Properties of Matter* in five volumes! Pagan nonsense!'' He knocked the books' dust from his hands and left the room. All grew still again, except for the breathing of the fire at Nonesuch's back. He looked at the flames.

You may know that if you stare long enough at a fire you can see many different shapes in it. Sometimes the flames look like groves of trees or standing lines of people. They may seem to rise from burning houses or burning cities. The sparks look like snowflakes falling upwards. The upper levels of the fire can seem to move like flocks of birds. Or, if you look very closely, you can imagine you see small dragons hovering and dancing in the flames.

This was what Nonesuch saw now: a dragon in the flames, indeed a dragon that was part of the flames, so that it was impossible to say where the flames ended and its body began. Though the dragon's shape stayed the same as it flew happily back and forth, its size did change. In the yellow, or least hot, part of the flame the dragon was smallest. When it flew to the hottest, blue zone of the flame it grew, so that its wings spanned almost three inches.

Nonesuch watched the dragon for some time without daring to speak. If he did so, he thought, she might blend completely into the flames and vanish. She was more sprightly than he had ever seen her: as happy as only a creature can be that has found its true element. But she looked infinitely old too, glowing wisely in the fire, with an eye so bright that Nonesuch could scarcely look at it.

"Hello, Grandmother," he said at last.

His grandmother did not answer him immediately; but he could tell from the expression on her face, from the way that her flight became more elegant and precise, that she knew he was there. Indeed, she must have known it before he saw her. She had been waiting for him to speak. She hovered skilfully over a burning coal, flapping her wings to settle down on it. "So, here we are again, you and I, just as in the old days." She nodded towards the back of the fireplace, which, Nonesuch now saw, was of rough stone, arched like the roof of a cavern.

But it wasn't really as in the old days, he thought. They had both changed, he in his way almost as much as she. Many years had passed since their days in the cavern above Serpent Grimsby, and many adventures. He had been out in the world of men, in that very world his grandmother had so distrusted. Now, he thought, there were things he could teach her, if she would only listen to him. But he kept his voice very respectful as he replied, ''Not exactly the same: I'm a good deal older now.''

''And wiser too,'' his grandmother answered. ''I can see that for myself. Though not as wise as you might be.'' She chuckled, with a silvery, hissing sound.

Nonesuch decided to let that comment pass for the present. His grandmother might think otherwise soon. ''How did you come here, Grandmother?'' he asked.

Again she laughed. ''Oh, I can go anywhere now! Since the unimportant part of me was burned away, I am lighter than air. If I explained how I was made, you wouldn't understand it yet. I am only visible from inside a fire. You might think of me as pure flame; that would fit your present level of comprehension.''

''You can only live in fire?'' Nonesuch asked, distressed.

''I can only be *seen* in fire; I can live where I like. But I have seen enough from within fires too; there was a change of religion in this country a few years ago – not to bore you with the details – and humans tend to burn each other at such times.''

His grandmother became very thoughtful. ''One occasion sticks in my mind,'' she said, flying upward again while her red eyes shone. ''Two old men in long robes, whom they burned by the grey walls of Oxford, their seat of learning as they called it; they had learned to burn each other there, at least. The old men could have run away, it seemed, or said some words that would have saved themselves. But they would do neither. That would not have been consistent with their natures. They almost welcomed the fire. One of them told the other to be brave, because they would light such a candle together that it would never be put out. I wondered what he meant.

"They were both true and brave, I thought. I was almost tempted to turn the fire aside for them — though they wouldn't have liked that. If they had seen me, they would have taken me for their Devil.

"But I found that all this was filling my mind with too many thoughts of humans; since then I've kept away from them. I've avoided their traps. I've travelled light."

Very light indeed, Nonesuch thought. His grandmother had become a creature without any substance that he could understand.

"I *can* turn fire aside, you know," she added with modest pride. "See!" She spoke to the flames and they all roared up into a far corner of the fireplace, so that for a moment his grandmother disappeared. "When the flames were approaching this house, some years ago, I spoke to them and they turned aside. I didn't want you to be disturbed."

"I had a good sleep," Nonesuch said gratefully. "Besides that, you protected my treasure."

"That too," she told him. "Your book. You seem to be guarding it well, small as you are."

"You saw my book? How could you have seen it?"

Again his grandmother laughed. "I've been with you for a long time. I was there to watch your Brother Theophilus making your book." Nonesuch stared at her as she hovered in the flames. "That was a fine time you had, so close to humans. You took a great deal of trouble over them."

"I had to," Nonesuch told her stiffly. "They were *my* people."

"Careful there! You'll have more than enough to do if you

go on that way. But you left them behind in the end. You flew away in time, like a proper dragon.''

Nonesuch thought of the people he had known. ''I was sorry to leave them,'' he said at last.

''There's no need to be sorry. There will be others and much the same. Humans do tend to repeat themselves over the centuries. There's no end of them, but only a few dragons.''

Nonesuch looked away to consider what she had said. His eye was caught by the picture on the wall, the picture that showed a dragon eating its own tail. ''What dragon is that?'' he asked.

His grandmother stared at the picture and hissed angrily. ''*That* is no dragon at all!'' she snapped. ''That stupid picture represents a misconception of the alchemists, a seedy bunch even for humans. I spent some time in one of their 'laboratories', and I can tell you that you have never seen such muddlers, such incompetents.''

She looked again at the picture of the dragon eating its own tail with such fury and fire in her eyes that Nonesuch almost expected to see the picture burst into flame. ''They said that dragons represented the material, imperfect part of matter that had to be destroyed to change 'base' metals such as lead into 'noble' ones like gold.'' His grandmother hissed. ''Can you imagine *humans* regarding dragons as imperfect?

''No,'' his grandmother told Nonesuch, who by this time was perched on the dog-headed fire-iron, listening to her with as complete attention as he had done long ago in the cavern, ''we dragons know about the nature of matter. We know that matter is nothing, unless there is a dragon to watch it. Now I have mingled so with the elements that I begin to understand their ways. I suppose I could change lead into gold if I saw any reason to do so.

"Indeed," she continued, "we have a story that once all matter was much denser than gold, denser than you can imagine: so that all the universe occupied a space smaller than this fireplace. And there was a dragon who watched it all. In time, so the story goes, this dragon grew bored with so much density and let the matter expand to its present form. The results have been interesting. I suspected all this before my change and have learned much more of it since. But now we have started to grow tired of such a thin and frivolous state of matter: for we are a restless breed, we dragons, never really satisfied; we love change for its own sake. Now and then we return stars to their original compact state. Things seem more tidy that way. Soon it may be time for your galaxy as well."

It took Nonesuch another moment to realize what she was saying. "And our earth?" he asked her.

"It is part of the galaxy, I believe," his grandmother replied primly. "A very small part."

"And the humans on it too?"

"Of course." His grandmother seemed surprised that he should ask.

"I wouldn't like that," Nonesuch told her.

His grandmother stared at him, concerned. "You *have* become too fond of them! It's a natural reaction, I suppose; but you'll get over it. They're of little account, really. Occasionally their minds seem to aim at wisdom, but they are too much creatures of the flesh ever to reach it."

"They are often kind to each other," Nonesuch told her.

His grandmother sniffed. "So are rabbits."

"They help each other; they work together."

"Usually for no good purpose."

"But they can help each other; and the poor, too."

"If you are thinking of your abbey, at Oddfields, or whatever its name was," Nonesuch's grandmother replied, "it is no longer there. One of their kings turned the monks out of all the abbeys and gave their gold and property to his followers. It was his older daughter, the one they called Bloody Mary, who burned my two old men and so many others to make amends for her father's crimes."

Nonesuch did not answer immediately, thinking of the abbey. "They make beautiful things," he said at last. Perhaps it was still true.

His grandmother did not seem to be in a mood to give humans credit for anything. "Only because they are not content with the world as it is," she told him. "They want to prop up their own vanity."

"Their church windows make the light more beautiful."

"If you like that sort of thing," his grandmother retorted. "Personally, I find their stained glass full of simple-minded fables and naive symbols."

"They cut stones that hover in the air like fountains of water."

"They should have left the stones where they belonged, in the earth. I have crawled through veins of marble, through galleries of stalactites and stalagmites, more beautiful than a hundred palaces."

"They make books," Nonesuch told his grandmother.

She spread her wings and fanned the coal beneath her. She did not reply immediately. "Ha!" she said. "Your book, for example."

"And many others."

"They do that, I admit," his grandmother said. "For what final purpose I am not sure." She paused again, swelling and shrinking in the flames. "So you are fond of your book?"

"It is the most beautiful thing in the world," Nonesuch told her.

"Perhaps the only beautiful one that humans have made," said his grandmother. "Still, as you are so fond of it, you should keep it. I'll pass the word that you are not to be disturbed for a time." She looked at him for a long moment. "There is another saying: 'A true dragon always remains with what he loves; if he can.' "

As she sat there in the flames, thinking deeply, the door of the laboratory opened. A tall man in a long blue coat with gold buttons, wearing a thick wig and thick spectacles, entered. He looked at the bubbling flasks and opened a draft in a brazier to adjust the heat under one of them. He sniffed at the liquid in a bottle and wrote down something in a black notebook.

The grandmother watched him with close attention until he had left the room. "Your new gentleman is an amateur," she told Nonesuch. "He will learn nothing new. But he is in for a nasty surprise. Though the terms haven't been invented yet, he is generating hydrogen and oxygen gases in those flasks. They combine violently to make water when given the chance. They have all the chance in the world with these open flames. I think you had better be inside your box when the combination occurs."

She left the coal bed and hovered halfway up the fireplace. "Definitely, you should go back to your box and stay there," she told Nonesuch. "You may hear some noise and commotion: stay in your box. There will be even less to see outside than there is now."

His grandmother rose in the flames, while Nonesuch followed her lovingly with his eyes. As she reached the upper levels she began to fade. She hovered there a moment more so that he could still watch her; then, with a wink, she vanished.

# CHAPTER XI

# THE BOOKSHOP

# IS GRANDMOTHER HAD BEEN WISE TO INSIST THAT

Nonesuch stay in his box. The explosion occurred the very next day. The blast swept the table clean. The brazier, the flask, and all its attachments were thrown against the wall. Acrid smoke filled the room, seeped into Nonesuch's box, and made him sneeze. He heard shouts and running footsteps. There was a sound of blows and flapping as men beat out the flames, of scraping as burning fragments of wood were gathered and tossed into the fireplace. Shutters were flung apart, and the door was opened and shut rapidly to drive away the smoke.

After a time new footsteps entered the room. Nonesuch recognized the steps of the man in brown who had carried in the books and of the bewigged man whom his grandmother had called an amateur. This one spoke first. ''It was a damned near thing, Angus! I might have been in the room myself, or any of us.''

''It was God's mercy, sir,'' Angus replied.

The master's footsteps walked up and down the room, crunching glass heavily. ''I'll tell you what, Angus,'' he said at last. ''Some excitement is very well, but this has ceased to be amusing.'' He sniffed at the air. ''A frightful stink — but it really wasn't so much better at other times. They noticed it at Court. The wits have had some profit from it at my expense.'' He sniffed again, loudly. ''Well, they'll profit no more!'' Glass crackled under his feet as he turned to look around the room. ''This chemistry is a disorderly nonsense! Nothing will come of it.''

Angus coughed politely. The master continued, ''This episode has decided me on a more gentlemanly occupation.''

''Indeed, sir.'' Angus's voice was grateful.

''But they'll hear of it all the same,'' the master said in a moment. ''How they'll laugh! I'll have to shun my coffee-houses as well.''

Angus coughed gently. ''Perhaps if you were away for a time, sir. Your friends will find some new diversion.''

There was another pause. ''That's true,'' the master said at last. ''I have been neglecting my proper concerns. I had a letter from Scotland, from the steward at Kilprankie, about repairs to the stables. I should go there myself and see to it. And you too, of course, since you understand the humdrum details better than I. You wouldn't mind that, I imagine.''

''Indeed, sir,'' Angus said, ''the country air would do you a world of good.'' He paused, then coughed. ''And the equipment?''

''All destroyed, I should imagine.''

''There are no glass bottles intact, sir. But the flasks are only a wee bit damaged. And the balance and mortars were sheltered somewhat from the blast.''

''I have no interest in any of them now! They can be thrown into the Thames, for what I care.''

"That would be a waste, sir," Angus said respectfully.

The master chuckled. "Hm, still clinging to your Highland ways, I see. Well, do as you like. But get them from my sight."

Angus said, after another pause, "They'll never be noticed in the stable storeroom at Kilprankie, sir."

"Whatever you want; I leave such details to you."

"I'll see to cleaning all this up, sir," Angus told him.

"The sooner the better."

Both men left the room. Others entered, and in a short time Nonesuch felt himself moving again. His box, with the flask still attached, was placed in the bottom of a large crate. A second flask, whose supporting blocks had been burned away, was also placed in the crate, together with books and other pieces of laboratory equipment. The crate was nailed shut.

While all this was going on, and later, when the crate was loaded on a wagon and taken to the gentleman's country estate fifty miles north of Edinburgh, Nonesuch stayed inside his own box. He was aware of the wagon's movements; he could feel the roads grow rougher and more hilly as they travelled north. He could hear the drivers talking and the voices of stable-boys in inns along the way. These voices changed from sharp London tones to slower, broader accents and later to Scots accents like that of Angus, the steward, who was riding ahead of both his master and the luggage to see that all would be proper at the Kilprankie estate.

At last, one day the crate was lifted out of the wagon. Nonesuch smelled the smoke of a peat fire and the sweat of the two men who were carrying the crate. "Ach!" said the one in front, "mair o' the maister's London nonsense!"

"Patience there, Sandy," an older voice from the rear replied. "He won't bide here long to trouble us. You maun just bear it."

The men set the crate down and walked away, chuckling

together. The room became very still. Nonesuch left his box, crawled through the packed laboratory equipment, and looked out the side of the crate. He saw a storeroom, with farm implements and a stack of faded brown carpet from which two earwigs were advancing towards him. There seemed to be nothing outside worth examining, he thought, and he had better guard his own book.

In a short while he slept again. In the country stillness, with only the sound of wind over the fields or a distant neigh from the stables, he slept deeply.

It was long before he so much as dreamed again. Then, it was a strange dream indeed. He found himself in a large room, lit with bright hanging globes such as he had never seen before. In the centre was a long table piled with objects of all kinds, including his own box with the flask still attached. A man stood at one end of the table calling out numbers. A thick crowd of people filled the room. Some waved white cards, others called out numbers too. The tones of their voices were different from those Nonesuch remembered, though some reminded him of the voice of the steward, Angus, who was not there. Nonesuch's grandmother was in the room, though, perched happily on one of the globes, whose light shone through her. "You've come to the right place!" she hissed at him. "A number here or there will decide your fate!"

While Nonesuch tried to understand this strange statement, his dream changed again. Now he was flying high in the air, so high that at first he mistook the clouds beneath him for snow on the ground. Air rushed past with a smooth hiss, though he did not feel the wind on his skin. This could happen only in a dream, he thought. He could see no humans or their buildings. When the clouds cleared away, he found himself still flying, but over an endless sheet of wrinkled grey-blue water. He saw a queer boat very far below. Its wake showed it was moving along, but it had no sails, unlike the ships he had seen in his own early days. Far off to one side, going in the opposite direction, was a flying creature – another dragon, he thought with a thrill. But this one flew without moving its wings at all. As distant as it was, he realized it was much larger than any dragon he had ever seen. How could such a large one have survived this long?

Even though he reminded himself that it was all a dream, this last thought disturbed Nonesuch greatly. Had he been wrong to grow so small? It was comforting when thick clouds came around him again and the dream left him to his deep slumber.

But the reality when he truly woke was stranger still. He opened his eyes. Bright daylight, shining through a clear window, had slipped between the pages of his book. A fresh, salty breeze was blowing between them as well. For the first time in hundreds of years, Nonesuch smelled the sea. But it was a different smell from that of the sea that had washed the beaches south of Serpent Grimsby, or that had broken on the rocky islands by the coast of Scotland. The seaweed, the dried driftwood, and the fish scales were not quite the same. And there was another smell unlike any that he had encountered before: one that he came to recognize later as motor oil from the boats in the marina just offshore.

But he had no time to sort out these odors now. There were humans close by, three of them. His book was out of its box, and one of the humans had just turned over a page! How many more were still above him? Nonesuch flattened himself down and slipped sideways so that he lay between two branches of a vine. If the page above him was lifted, he might be mistaken for a painted dragon there.

''Beautiful!'' It was an old man's voice. The accent was

quite new to Nonesuch, but not the tone of enthusiasm, which he found strangely comforting.

A clear woman's voice, also old, said, "And you got this at an *auction*? Did you mortgage the whole shop to pay for it?"

"Twenty-five pounds," the old man's voice replied proudly.

"I don't believe you. The Scots are not so stupid."

"Not for the book. For the box, and its attachments."

A young man's voice was heard. "You should have seen Dad in action!" He waited for the older man to speak, then continued. "I wanted the flask, even though it was damaged. But someone else was bidding for it too; a little dry fellow, a pharmacist, I think. We got to ten pounds, but he still seemed stubborn. The bidding went to fifteen. Then Dad touched my elbow. He had been looking at the table and had seen something I had missed. He said, 'I'll add a bit for the box,' and called out, 'Twenty-five pounds.' That shut the pharmacist up, and it was all ours. The pharmacist was shaking his head at this extravagance. After all, perfect specimens of these flasks were listed in catalogues for forty pounds. Who would pay more than fifteen for a damaged one? I gave Dad a look as if to say, what are you doing? He whispered, 'You can have the flask; I'll just take the box.' "

The older man said, "I had noticed the ironwork round the box, under the paint. I thought, if someone had wanted to guard a box so carefully, there might be something in it."

"We had to rush to catch the plane at Glasgow," the young man said.

The woman sniffed. "I suppose that in your rush you didn't have time to buy any books at the auction — books that weren't in boxes?"

The older man said, "Peter picked up the remains of a

treatise on alchemy — in very poor condition. They had all come out of a storeroom in some decayed manor-house. All the books were in shreds. The beetles had gotten at them. I wonder how this one escaped. It was in a box, but that probably wouldn't have protected it from a really determined insect.''

The young man said, ''There just wasn't anything else. But Dad only had eyes for the box. He didn't like to ship it in his suitcase. If he hadn't been carrying the porcelain, he'd have taken it to his seat on the plane. He said he wanted to get it home before he opened it.''

''I had a feeling,'' the older man remarked.

''*You* opened it?'' the woman asked.

''I got Bartholomew to do it. Even he had a hard time. He said, 'They don't make locks like this now. They have no respect for the dignity of labor. Where did you get it?' But I didn't tell him. I carried it back without an explanation. I didn't want to open it anywhere else but here. I hope he didn't think I was rude. I'll give him that Italian edition of Lenin's letters.''

Another page of the book was turned. Nonesuch crouched lower still. ''The pages seemed warped,'' the old man remarked. ''Should I press them? I'll read about it before I do anything.''

''And I only wanted the flask,'' the younger man said.

''The flask you can have. Let it be my gift.''

''It's eighteenth-century,'' the younger man protested.

''Practically modern. *This* is fifteenth-century. A Book of Hours. It seems all to have been done by one hand.''

A small bell jingled. The three people stopped talking. A door swung open and a boy's voice said, ''Where are they?'' A stronger breeze from the open door lifted the page above Nonesuch just a fraction. He raised his head and saw that his book was on a wide table that ended near a layer of shelves, no more than a foot away from him, filled with more books than he had imagined possible. The sunlight that filled the room still left the depths of the nearest shelf in shadow. Nonesuch crawled to the edge of the page and looked sideways. An adjoining table was covered with paperback books stacked in rows, their spines upwards.

The newcomer, a plump, cheerful boy with his hair in all directions, wore a black T-shirt with a picture of a spaceship and a satellite circling the planet Saturn. He had placed a pile of schoolbooks on an empty part of the table and was stacking paperback books on these. The two men and the woman were standing with their backs to Nonesuch, close to the boy, as if to shield him from the sight of Nonesuch's book.

Now! The little dragon crouched at the edge of his book and sprang into the air. In all this time, his wings had not forgotten how to fly. In a moment he was deep inside the bookcase, well hidden, and able to survey the whole room.

The boy left with a large pile of books clutched between his arms and his chin. The woman held the door open for him, but he stumbled at the threshold; books tumbled round his feet.

"Careful, Samson," the woman said. She helped him pile up the books again and steered him carefully out the door.

"He seems to devour them," the older man remarked. "I'm afraid he'll run out of food soon."

"He read all our comic books," the woman explained to the young man, "including the annotated Krazy Kat. Now he's going through all the science-fiction we have. I wonder what he'll try next."

"He'll find something," the older man said. "But we'd better close up temporarily." He locked the door.

Nonesuch watched these new humans with deep attention

from the depths of his bookcase. The older man was tall, and partly bald, with a neat fringe of white hair and gold spectacles. The woman had thick grey-blonde hair, tied back in a bun. The young man was dark-haired, and unlike either of them. He had a busy look about him and soon left, saying he had to prepare his lecture.

The woman locked the door behind him. He climbed into a green closed wagon that could be seen through the wide windows of the room. Nonesuch was astonished to hear it start to roar and then to see it roll away by itself. The white-haired man did not turn his head at the departure of the Volkswagen Beetle. He continued to turn over the pages of Nonesuch's book, so carefully, and with a look of such respect and concentration, that the dragon had an unexplainable urge to fly out of the bookcase and perch on his shoulder.

The woman had come to watch the book too. ''He liked dragons,'' she remarked.

''Yes, didn't he?''

''They seem friendly. Or at least, diffident,'' the woman said.

''Most of them, yes. But look at this one. See how he's watching the man in the trees. Measuring him for his coffin, I'd say.''

''Or for his own lunch,'' the woman remarked. Both laughed and continued to study Nonesuch's book.

While they are doing so, and while Nonesuch is watching them, it is appropriate to tell the reader more about these people. You will have understood, of course, that we are now in the present day, quite late in the twentieth century. We are somewhere on the northeast coast of North America, in a city whose population is between 50,000 and 200,000. But I will not give the name of the city, or even of the bookshop, though

DISTANT VOYAGES, as it will be called from now on, is a close approximation. If people knew where the bookshop is to be found, too many of them might want to visit it; and this, as will become clear later, would not be at all desirable. So, let us just say that in a certain city was a certain bookstore. The owner, Mr. Samuel Gottlieb, had lived there, in an apartment above the bookshop, for some years with his wife, Ingrid, and their daughter, Rachel.

The building that now housed the bookshop had originally been a chandler's shop, for outfitting sailing ships in the harbor, which lay at the foot of a steep slope one hundred feet below. The road from the harbor zigzagged up this hill around small blue-and-white houses that perched bravely on the slope. In time, the lower part of the hill had been excavated and a new line of shops built, closer to the water. Among them was another chandler's shop that had taken over all the business. Thus, Mr. Gottlieb had been able to buy this one, together with the apartment above it. He kept a few of the ropes, fishnets, belaying pins, and grappling hooks for ornaments and filled the rest of the shop with books.

From its door, he had a fine view over the harbor, the wooded hills of the shoreline, and three small, rocky islands. Customers browsing among the books could look at the ships — mostly freighters now, but a few sailing vessels as well, and any number of small motor boats — and think of distant lands. There was always some unexpected book to be found on the shelves. Casual visitors to the shop tended to stay a long time and usually took a few books away with them.

When Rachel completed her studies at the university in the city behind the harbor, she decided to stay with her parents and work in the bookshop. She sent out detailed lists of their old travel books and built up a substantial mail-order business. Several customers came to the city to examine books from the list at first hand.

A frequent customer was Peter Levy, a young assistant professor of chemistry at the university. He came there first in search of books on the history of science, a subject that he had begun to study in depth. After he had seen all the books, he still came to see the bookseller's daughter. They had been married three months before, in March, when Peter Levy could not get away for a long honeymoon. When the term ended, Rachel's parents had treated the young couple to a trip to England.

Mr. Gottlieb had gone over too, separately of course, to investigate the books in a couple of estates that were for sale. He had always loved England, from the year he had spent there on his way west from Germany in 1939. Peter Levy had become deeply interested in the history of chemistry – a subject on which, later, he built his academic career – and was especially fascinated by old equipment. When, in Edinburgh, he had heard of the sale, by auction, of the contents of an old laboratory, including the books, he called his father-in-law in London.

Nonesuch learned all this in the next few weeks from hearing his humans talk as he made himself at home in the bookshop. After the discovery of Brother Theophilus's book, Mr. Gottlieb could hardly be bothered with anything else. He kept the book in his office, to which he had added a new lock. He would sit over it for hours. Peter Levy came often too and examined the book with great interest. Once he approached the pages with a small scalpel. Mr. Gottlieb look worried. Nonesuch, who had found a good hiding-place within the crammed pigeon-holes of an old desk, bristled. But Peter only removed a tiny scrap of paint from a vine, where it did not show, and took it away in a test-tube.

He reported next day, ''The gas-liquid chromatograph showed it couldn't have been made after 1500.''

''I knew that,'' Mr. Gottlieb said.

''The pattern of lipids was very definite,'' Peter added. ''If you could spare a bit of one page, I could do some carbon dating.''

''Never mind,'' said Mr. Gottlieb. ''But I'm glad your measurements confirm my judgement.'' When he left the office, he locked the book in an old maple cabinet.

It disturbed Nonesuch to see his book shut away so, but he soon found that there were enough cracks in the back of the cabinet for him to slip through and lie down among the book's pages.

Now his periods of sleep were very short. Mr. Gottlieb might disturb him at any hour of the day or night. Often he padded downstairs from the apartment in his dressing-gown and slippers, a large cup of tea in his hand. He would take the book from its cupboard, spread it out on his desk under a bright light, and study the pages, writing detailed comments in a red notebook.

One day, Peter Levy came with a camera and tripod and a set of bright lights. He photographed all the pages of the book. Later, he proudly showed the color prints to his father-in-law. ''Very impressive,'' Mr. Gottlieb said politely. ''Now you can study it too.'' Nonesuch could tell from his voice that the photographs interested him much less than the original. This pleased the little dragon, who had been curious about the copies, and had seen in them yet another example of the new, shiny things of the world to which he had now come. But he had realized immediately that such images could never replace the real book.

"But keep these to yourself and Rachel, if you please," Mr. Gottlieb told his son-in-law. "For the time being, the book will be a family secret." Nonesuch, crouched in his bookcase, well hidden in the shadows, nodded in approval of the book-seller's wisdom.

# CHAPTER XII

# A VIEW OF THE HARBOR

# T FIRST, NONESUCH PLANNED ALWAYS TO STAY NEAR HIS

book, but he soon realized that this was not necessary. He kept a close eye on Mr. Gottlieb and quickly became convinced that the bookseller was guarding his book almost as jealously as he. Then the dragon began to study the ways of the shop and of the world outside it. He soon learned to watch for the movement of the hands of the old wall clock: at ten every morning Mr. or Mrs. Gottlieb opened the bookshop doors.

Usually the first customer was Samson, the boy Nonesuch had seen on his first day. His school was only two blocks away, at the top of the hill, and he often visited the bookshop at recess. As Mr. Gottlieb had said, Samson was at present eating his way through science-fiction books, up to three an evening. He had read almost all the shop's small stock of these books. By special arrangement, he was permitted to bring back within a week any books he didn't want to keep. Even so, up to the present he had kept enough to use up all his allowance. He paid for the others by running errands, especially taking books to be mailed to the post office on the other side of his school. This was very helpful, since Mr. Gottlieb's leg had been troubling him and he didn't like to take his car for such a short distance. It was Mrs. Gottlieb who had suggested putting the boy on a small salary.

In the morning there also came mothers on the way home from the supermarket on top of the hill. They pushed shopping carts or baby buggies, which they left outside the door while they selected books on child care or gardening or vegetarian cookery or political science. At noon someone was sure to come in to buy a book to read while eating lunch at the restaurant next door. Now that the weather was fine, you could see them reading at the tables set out on the sidewalk, or across the road on the parapet overlooking the harbor.

Nonesuch soon learned to recognize other regular customers. There was a short, grey woman who lived in a small apartment in the city and bought books on formal gardening. A lecturer at the university often came to look for works of British explorers of Africa; a garage mechanic was building up his collection of books on old cars. Then there was Professor Ash.

Nonesuch had, of course, taken care that no one saw him. He understood very well that the sight of him would cause much more commotion than in the days when he had first entered his book. Fortunately there were many good hiding-places. In most of the shelves, there were gaps where books had been removed, and he could stay well back in the shadows. He found hidden roads between rows of books. Many shelves were built against the walls, but not too snugly: it was easy to pass from one level to another. Some free-standing shelves with double rows of books, however, were open on both sides. In these, he had to be especially careful to move only when no humans were near by.

He thought he was doing this. But late one morning when the shop was quiet, Mr. Gottlieb was in his office, and Mrs. Gottlieb was cutting the leather in her back room to cover a tattered nineteenth-century diary from Newfoundland, Nonesuch worked his way across from one side of a double shelf to the other; then, thinking himself quite alone, he flew across to the next standing shelf. There was a flash of eyes beneath him. He crouched, turned, and looked quickly down the wedge-shaped gap between two books.

A large, bearded man, his vest covered with ashes, was sitting on the floor between the shelves, an open book in his hand. The man kept staring up, so that daylight was reflected in his eyes; then he closed them and said, "*Now* I'm seeing dragons!" He reached into a baggy side pocket of his old tweed jacket and pulled out a flat bottle, one-third full. He shook it, looked at it sadly, and thrust it back again. Then he rose, grunting, and shuffled out of the shop.

Nonesuch learned to watch out for this man who could sit so quietly in one place. He kept completely out of sight when he smelt his odor of old tobacco smoke and whisky; but he watched him with great interest. He heard the Gottliebs talking about the bearded man, whom they called "Professor Ash". He had been a distinguished scholar, Mr. Gottlieb told his son-in-law. He still was: his knowledge of myths and legends was profound. But he had published little; he could never write down what he knew in a way that satisfied him. He had taken to drink years ago, lost his university position, and retired on a very small pension. Now he spent his time acquiring more knowledge in the city library or at this bookshop. He would sit in an old chair in the corner or, as now, on the floor for hours.

When he had had a drink or two from his pocket flask, Professor Ash had enough sense to close his eyes and pretend to be sleeping. At such times, Mr. Gottlieb would not disturb him. Indeed, he said he often thought of hanging a ''Do not disturb'' sign on the old man's broad shoulders. And sometimes Professor Ash really did sleep, and he dreamed about books.

Occasionally Mrs. Gottlieb looked at him critically, for he never bought any books, though he sometimes sold them some. Mr. Gottlieb would say mildly, ''Leave him alone; he knows where all our books are. He can even give me the prices, as if he had a catalogue in his head.'' His wife could only nod in agreement.

Nonesuch learned how much confidence Mr. Gottlieb had in Professor Ash when he called the old man into his office at the end of a day and showed him Nonesuch's book. ''Oh yes,'' Professor Ash said, running his fingertips over the pages. ''A treasure indeed.''

Mr. Gottlieb turned over another page. ''Here are more dragons,'' he said. ''I wonder why he painted so many dragons.''

''Perhaps he saw them,'' Professor Ash replied. He looked closely at the page. ''What's this in the vines, his signature? I can't make out the words.''

''Let me see.'' Mr. Gottlieb pushed his glasses up to his forehead and bent over the page. ''It says, 'Theophilus fecit.' ''

''Theophilus made the book, eh?'' Professor Ash commented. ''Theophilus means 'Lover of God', almost the same as your name.''

''That's right,'' said Mr. Gottlieb, very pleased.

No one besides the old professor had seen Nonesuch, and he was all the more careful to keep himself hidden. He stuck to the dark, shadowy places where he — no bigger than a large cockroach, now that he had eaten a few such insects — could conceal himself.

But hiding was easy really: his humans had their thoughts on other things. Mr. Gottlieb would know, without counting, if one of a twenty-volume set of the short stories of Anton Chekhov was missing, but he would not really notice if his socks did not match. He could not count on Mrs. Gottlieb to remind him, either, since she was often immersed in books about calligraphy or techniques of bookbinding. She had a small bookbinding press in the tiny room behind the shop where books were unpacked, and spent much of her time there. She was the most likely one to see Nonesuch, since she had taken on the responsibility of dealing with any insects in the shop, though not on an individual basis. She had been attacking these hated destroyers with roach powder, but shortly after Nonesuch's arrival, there were no roaches to eat the powder. "Where did all my clients go?" she would ask, puzzled.

If he was discreet, he would be safe enough inside the shop, Nonesuch thought. He could start to examine his surroundings. Naturally, he had looked into some of the books, but this was not easy. Most were so tight in their shelves that it was impossible to crawl between their pages. Those that were loose enough for him to force his way in included a Mexican cookbook, which he did not understand, and a good edition of *Treasure Island*, which was much more interesting. However, he could only read as quickly as he could move, and he found it very frustrating to follow the story so slowly.

When he was sure that all was in order in the bookshop, Nonesuch decided to explore the outside world. At first, leaving the building presented some problems. The door was locked at night, and he did not dare fly through it in daylight. He carefully examined the inside walls and at last found a promising crack, above a row of dusty early-twentieth-century romantic novels at the top of the tallest bookcase. Through this crack, Nonesuch could squeeze to the open air, just above the bookshop's sign.

Directly below him was the road, then a flagstone terrace that ended in a low stone wall. The ground dropped so steeply beyond the wall that a flat green rooftop with a flapping clothesline seemed to be directly below. Beneath the clothesline, two girls in bikinis were sunning themselves on a blanket. Other rooftops appeared at different levels on the hill, some flat, most peaked, with worn, glowing brick chimneys.

To the left, past a row of tables with red-checked cloths that were set out on the terrace, the hill withdrew from the shore. Nonesuch looked down on a small business district with a park and a shopping mall.

But the more distant scene soon commanded his attention. As Nonesuch looked at the harbor spread out before him, he stayed for a long time crouched on the sign, moving nothing but his head to take it all in. He saw two freighters riding at anchor and another one docked beneath a huge crane on rails that was piling on containers as if they had been blocks of wood. A few motor boats moved about like water-bugs on a pond. Further out, two sailboats, one with red and one with blue sails, were chasing each other round a small island.

Evening was falling; a flight of swallows dotted the windy air. At last Nonesuch spread his wings and joined them. The swallows, rising on a draft from the harbor, looked at him curiously but continued swooping and snapping up insects. One swallow turned to snap at him too, then flew quickly away, leaving two of its tail feathers floating. Nonesuch glided far out until he was past the hill and over the water. Now he saw that the bookshop was the middle one of three plain two-storey buildings. To the right of the bookshop, as he faced it, was a small restaurant with a wide new picture window and a sign, THE BALCONY (formerly THE SAILOR'S REST). On the other side of the bookshop was a shop with a door in the centre, and a window on one side full of shoes and on the other side, of locks and bolts. A sign above the door read, B. SACCO, THE GOOD SHOEMAKER (ALSO KEYS).

The low sun shone past the front windows and glowed on the face of a small, wrinkled man who sat at a bench hammering away at the heel of a shoe with deep concentration. On the sidewalk in front of him was a large grey parrot, tethered to a perch.

The parrot turned his head so that the setting sun flashed up from his bill into Nonesuch's eye. The bird's eye flashed too, with such a look of wisdom that in a short time Nonesuch flew down and lighted on the window molding above the parrot's head.

The parrot tilted his head again and looked at the dragon for a long time. "Did you come on a banana boat?" he asked at last.

Nonesuch took his own time in answering. "Hardly," he said.

"You have something of a jungle look about you," the parrot explained. "All sorts of tropical creatures come in on the ships: tarantulas, even small boas; I don't know what all. Usually, they die in the cold weather, so I hear. You should take care to keep warm."

"I do," Nonesuch told him.

The parrot nodded. "I don't want to give unsolicited advice," he assured Nonesuch. "I can't get the jungle out of my mind. Sitting here, with this northern sea and sky, I still recall the damp, green, rotten jungles of the Amazon River where I was hatched, a green world as it must have been at the beginning of time, with more forms of life than you can imagine. That's what I knew when I was very small, before I was captured and lived among men and learned human speech.''

Nonesuch flew quickly out over the road to look inside the shop again at the man bent over his shoe. "Did he capture you?" he asked the parrot.

"No, indeed," the parrot said. "He would never have done that. I was taken by an Indian boy. He carried me and my brothers to market inside a dried calabash. I was purchased by a young missionary at the very end of the market day. Often I have wondered what happened to my brothers: if they were also sold the next day, or set free, or left to dry in the calabash. But my first master was good to me. I learned much of their Bible as he read it aloud to himself in the jungle. Later he fell ill and had to return to England. He gave me to his housekeeper, who had seemed so fond of me, but who sold me immediately to a sailor.

"That was my present master, Mr. Sacco. He took me with him on his ship, the *Matilda McClintock*, where he was second engineer. We were torpedoed during the war, in the North Atlantic. He ran back to rescue me from his cabin before he would leave the ship, and he broke his leg jumping through the flames into a lifeboat. They set it badly in the boat, and he still limps."

The parrot sighed. "What a voyage that was! Icebergs came trundling down from the North Pole, cold castles that sneered at our little lifeboat. Snow squalls beat down on us;

we were in a white world without color or warmth. I kept Mr. Sacco's spirits up in the lifeboat with words my first master used to read: 'For thou didst cast me into the depth, in the heart of the seas. And the flood was round about me. All thy waves and billows passed over me.' I won't say all those verses cheered him up,'' the parrot added, ''but he seemed amused. One able seaman in the lifeboat would weep and say, 'A parrot quoting from Jonah! Next we'll see a whale.' We saw several, in fact, but they kept their distance. Ever since we were rescued, Mr. Sacco has kept me with him.''

Nonesuch looked at the parrot with new respect. ''Where was your war?'' he asked him.

''Oh, far away and years ago.''

Nonesuch nodded. ''I have seen human wars, too. I thought it was the only thing they could do. To get away from them you had to go to the forest, say to a quiet pool among the trees. But here they seem at peace together.'' He looked again at the boats moving around the harbor, keeping well away from each other. In the little business district below to the left, the lights were now turned on. People were strolling down the mall without fear. The automobiles moved in an orderly fashion, stopping at the traffic lights. Sounds of music reached them from a band in the park.

''So many of them,'' Nonesuch said, ''but I have seen no soldiers. They must have learned to live together after all this time.'' In fact, though he was not ready to tell the parrot so much of his own past, the scene all around him: the bookshop, the man at his bench repairing shoes, the few early customers at the restaurant tables reading by twilight, even the busy world below, reminded him of the Abbey of Oddfields. He saw Peter Levy, who must have just come into the bookshop, leave it together with Rachel. They crossed the road and sat on the stone parapet, facing the harbor, with their arms about each other.

The parrot cleared his throat. "Not to be a spoil-sport, but I doubt if my master would agree with you. He is a socialist. He'll talk to his customers for hours about the exploitation of one man by another. If he weren't such a good shoemaker, he'd lose all his business."

The parrot looked closely at Nonesuch. "And a good locksmith, too; the best. I've heard it said that there's no lock he can't open. Though he had some trouble two weeks ago with a box the bookseller brought to him. It was all very mysterious, that box and its contents. *You* wouldn't happen to know about it, by chance?"

Nonesuch kept a discreet silence. The parrot looked at him even more closely, but did not question him further. "By the way," he added, "if you're going to be in the neighborhood, watch out for the white cat from the restaurant. He's death on most birds and might mistake you for one. I've had to give him a few knocks with my bill to teach him a lesson."

"I've never had to bother with cats," Nonesuch told the parrot. Shortly afterwards, he flew back to the hole over the DISTANT VOYAGES sign and entered the bookshop again.

Samson was in the shop, looking over the table of science-fiction books with little interest. Professor Ash stuck his head out from between two bookcases. "Have you read them all?" he asked.

"Just about," Samson admitted. He pulled out a book from the middle row, looked at the back cover, and leafed through it. "Yechh!" he said.

"What's that one?" Professor Ash asked him.

Samson shrugged. *Conquest of the planet Adalbaran 12.* He turned over some more pages. "The natives don't like *anyone*," he explained. "They have anti-gravity rays and deep-penetrating lasers. The explorers have to set up force fields or they'll be made into inter-galactic chicken soup." He made a face. "It's all too easy: he writes down whatever he wants. It doesn't seem any harder than exploring the North Pole."

"That was easy?" Professor Ash asked him.

"Well, you didn't have to leave Earth to find it."

"Enough did. Here," Professor Ash said, "since you mention polar exploration, you might want to read about it." He reached behind him, without looking, and pulled a book from the shelf. "It deals with the Antarctic, which is an even more hostile region than the Arctic." He laid the book before Samson, who grimaced at its size but opened the cover.

"*The Worst Journey in the World*." He read the title with interest.

"The name refers to a winter journey the author took to collect penguin eggs," Professor Ash said. "He made the trip for the sake of knowledge, like all good explorers, and had to endure temperatures of seventy degrees below zero. He was young and strong and recovered from *that* journey. But his real worst journey was the trip he took later to find the bodies of Captain Scott, the leader of the whole Antarctic expedition, and his two companions, who froze on the way back from the South Pole just eleven miles from a fuel depot that might have saved their lives. To the end of his own life, the writer of *this* book blamed himself, unjustly, for failing to rescue them."

Samson picked up the book again, turned to the inside cover, and winced at the price. "I'll have to save up for this one," he remarked. He left the book, which remained open on the table. That night, Nonesuch started to read it, hovering over it, then crawling beneath the pages and walking towards the spine, with his back arched, to turn them over. He read the brave and tragic story of Scott's party, who arrived at the South Pole only to find that the Norwegian explorer Amundsen had already been there. He read, through Scott's journals, of the desperate journey back towards the base camp, all of them growing weaker on inadequate food and fuel. He read of "Titus" Oates, who, knowing he had no chance to reach the base camp and realizing he was a burden to his comrades, had deliberately walked out into the blizzard to die and give the others a chance.

But the chance came too late. Nonesuch carefully read Scott's last entries in his journal, which was found with his body. "Outside the door of the tent it remains a scene of whirling drift," he read. The words reminded him of the parrot's own winter journey, and of the cold white world he had seen; the parrot's account gave him more confidence in that of the human. Then he came to Scott's words, "We are weak, writing is difficult, but for my part I do not regret this journey, which has shown that Englishmen can endure hardships, help one another, and meet death with as great fortitude as ever in the past. We took risks, we knew we took them; things have come out against us, and therefore we have no cause for complaint, but bow to the will of Providence, determined still to do our best till the last. . . ." No, Nonesuch thought, carrying on a silent conversation with his grandmother, this was the way in which a dragon might speak. These humans seemed worth saving after all, even if one of them had not written his special Book of Hours. That evening, Mr. Gottlieb did not come downstairs to look at this book. When the dragon saw the sky outside begin to pale, he carefully, with some labor, turned the pages of *The Worst Journey in the World* back to their original position, slipped under the locked door to the office — fortunately, the door had warped enough to make this easy — and returned to his own sleeping-place in the cupboard.

# CHAPTER XIII

# Mr. Abercrombie

HE BOOK ON THE ANTARC-
TIC EXPLORERS REMAINED
on the table much of the next day. Nonesuch had hopes of continuing to read it that
evening. Towards the end of the afternoon,
however, a new customer entered the shop
and eventually took the book away with
him. This was a tall, distinguished, silver-
haired man who wore an elegant brown
cashmere sweater. His face was fresh and
smooth, and he smiled easily. For a time
after he entered, he stood just inside the
door, looking the books over. Nonesuch
bristled: the stranger seemed to be passing
his eyes over each book as if he were adding them all up, but with little interest in
their contents.

Mr. Gottlieb had been watching him too.
''Can I help you?'' he asked.

''Possibly,'' the stranger replied pleas-
antly. ''I was driving by and saw your little
corner.'' He continued to look around the
books, smiling. Then he leaned forward and
pulled one from a shelf. ''Foxe's *Booke of
Martyrs*,'' he announced.

''That's a good edition,'' Mr. Gottlieb
told him. ''It's abridged, of course. The original would fill up the whole shelf. There may
be a complete one at the university library.''

"I'm sure this will have the well-known passages." The stranger turned the pages. "Ah, here's old Bishop Latimer: 'Be of good cheer, Master Ridley, and play the man. We shall this day, by God's grace, light up such a candle in England as, I trust, will never be put out.' "

Nonesuch, who with trembling wings had been watching the stranger's every move, now froze with astonishment. His grandmother had described that very scene!

"Are you especially interested in that period?" Mr. Gottlieb asked him.

The stranger shook his head. "No more than in other times of idiocy. There's only a certain amount of interest in the reasons men burn each other." He looked at the book again. "How they did carry on!" He hummed a little tune. "Have you seen the place?"

"I'm afraid not."

"In Oxford, you know; by Balliol College. There's a cross there now; in a parking lot. If the taxis move, you can see the very spot."

That was where Nonesuch's grandmother had said the old men were burned: at Oxford. But why did the stranger find it so amusing?

"The old fools could have escaped, you know," the stranger said.

"Or renounced their faith," said Mr. Gottlieb. "They chose to do neither."

The stranger clicked his tongue. "Such stupidity."

The bookseller did not answer, and the stranger continued to read. His next words distressed Nonesuch. "Still, as you say, it seems a well-printed edition. I think I'll buy it."

Mr. Gottlieb coughed hastily. "I'm afraid that book is promised to someone else. I should have taken it off the shelf."

"Really!" The stranger smiled again. "I wouldn't have thought the subject would be so popular."

Mr. Gottlieb blushed. "A specialist in the wars of religion."

"Really?" The stranger pointedly looked away, to ignore the blush. "I really do want this book, you know."

Mr. Gottlieb shrugged, embarrassed.

"Well, in one way or another," the stranger said, almost to himself. His eyes fell on the book about the explorers of the Antarctic. He picked it up and turned over the pages. "Is this one also reserved, perhaps for a polar specialist?"

Mr. Gottlieb shook his head. The stranger turned to the price on the front cover. He extended a ten-dollar bill. "Then I'll have it."

Mr. Gottlieb dumbly accepted the money.

The stranger was in no hurry to leave. He continued to turn over the book's pages, still humming his little tune. "Death in a lonely tent," he remarked. "Of course, today he could see it all by airplane with little or no risk. What a wasted effort!"

"He thought the search for knowledge was worth while at the time, I believe," Mr. Gottlieb observed drily. "Others did too. They still do, in fact."

The stranger smiled. "Indeed. A romantic view but not a realistic one; especially considering that Scott's party arrived at the South Pole after Amundsen did. They needn't have gone at all." He looked at the book in his hand again and shook his head. "All these efforts that come to nothing: history is full of them. Inventors who have their work stolen. Poor mad Van Gogh, who hardly sold a single picture in his short life. How many art dealers has he made rich? It's better to be a dealer than a creator. You were wise to decide to be a dealer."

"Well," Mr. Gottlieb replied, "it wasn't so much a matter of wisdom. I have no special creative talents, though I admire them in others, more than anything else in fact. But I simply sell books. People seem to need them."

"How sensible to recognize your limitations," the stranger said. He added, "I wouldn't mind having an early copy of Scott's *Journal* if it comes your way. Or of the *Booke of Martyrs* if you find another copy or if your, uh, specialist on wars of religion doesn't call for it. Let me give you my card." He handed one to the bookseller. As it passed, Nonesuch could read the words "Brian Abercrombie".

"I live on Butcher's Point," the stranger added.

Mr. Gottlieb nodded. "You have a fine view there."

"Yes, of course." Mr. Abercrombie walked to the door and stopped, struck by the panorama before him. "But *you* have a view!" he exclaimed. He stepped out to the road, crossed it, and returned to the bookshop. "What space and what a location, just for the three of you! How could you have remained undiscovered for so long?"

"We're pretty well known locally," Mr. Gottlieb told him.

"Locally?" Mr. Abercrombie glanced round the empty shop. "I must leave you to your local customers."

But he did not leave immediately. He stayed a long time on the sidewalk, looking at the three buildings. He walked out to the parapet as well, studying the slope of the ground below, and walked past the restaurant to examine the hill behind it.

Mr. Gottlieb was still disturbed that evening. "Why did I make up that story?" he asked his wife. "What is it to me who buys my books? And he knew I was lying all the time."

"He sounds like a nasty piece of work," Mrs. Gottlieb remarked.

"More of a joker, I think," Mr. Gottlieb said, more tolerantly. His mind was again on Nonesuch's Book of Hours. He had been studying some of the marginal drawings. Here and there he had seen a kind of food chain in progress: a mouse ate a cricket and in turn was eaten by a cat, who was devoured by a wolf, who was shot by an archer, who was drowned and eaten by fishes. Sometimes the chain would be broken by the smaller creatures (but not the larger ones) escaping into the vines. These tiny stories calmed Mr. Gottlieb's spirit. "We probably won't hear from him again," he remarked, putting Mr. Abercrombie's card away in a file.

Because he was ashamed, Mr. Gottlieb did not mention his visitor to his daughter. The next day a new customer entered the shop when she was alone, except for Nonesuch, who was looking wistfully at the front of the *Booke of Martyrs*, which was too tightly wedged in place for him to peek inside. He had to scuttle behind the next book when this one was suddenly withdrawn from the shelf. He ran up the front of a book and looked out.

A stout man in a soiled, rumpled suit with broad blue stripes was holding out the book to Rachel. "This one," he said. Nonesuch saw him reach into a bulging pocket of his jacket and withdraw two pink gumdrops which he popped into his mouth.

"You'd like to buy this book?" Rachel asked doubtfully.

"That's the one."

Rachel bit her lip slightly but pulled out a sales slip from beneath the cash register. "What is your name, please?"

"Huberman," the fat man said.

Rachel wrote it down. "This is an unusual choice, Mr. Huberman," she observed.

"Isn't it for sale? It was on the shelf."

"Oh yes, it's for sale."

"So, I've bought it." Then the fat man smiled, showing discolored teeth. Rachel stepped back. "But not for myself."

"A present?" Rachel asked hopefully.

"For my employer," Huberman explained. "He has wide tastes. He said to tell you he was interested in the wars of religion. When he has an interest, any interest, he satisfies it. Did something hiss?"

Nonesuch, furious, backed away to the depths of the shelf.

"It must have been the wind," Rachel said.

"You should get it fixed," Huberman told her.

As he left the shop, Nonesuch left by his own route to follow him. Huberman drove away in an old black Buick, down the hill to the throughway along the coast. As Nonesuch watched from high in the air, he saw Mr. Abercrombie again, standing by two automobiles on a lookout point beside a smaller road. With him was another man who was examining the bookshop terrace with field-glasses. The dragon let Huberman go in order to watch this new pair. In a short while they separated; the man with the field-glasses, a jolly, balding fellow in a plaid coat, drove to the restaurant beside the bookshop, drank a soft drink on the terrace, then walked up and down carefully studying the hill behind the three buildings.

Two days later the bookseller received a call from a real estate agent asking him if he was interested in selling his building. No thank you, Mr. Gottlieb replied. A pity, the agent said: he had a client who was very interested in that part of the city and who would pay quite a good price. I like it here too, Mr. Gottlieb told the agent. Perhaps you'll be more interested in selling at a later time, the agent said politely.

Mr. Gottlieb would hardly have remembered the call, though it was the first such he had ever received, but he learned that on the two following days his neighbors had received similar calls: Mr. Sacco, the shoemaker, hearing from another real estate agent; and the owners of the restaurant, two widowed sisters who had married two brothers, from a lawyer. None of them were interested, they agreed. They were sitting, as was their custom on Friday evenings, on the restaurant terrace overlooking the harbor. Nonesuch had been out flying and, shortly before the humans came, had descended to the deep-green leaves of a lilac tree that hung over the table. He was no more than a yard from Mr. Gottlieb's nose and was able to hear everything that was said.

"The very idea!" said Mrs. Amanda Pickersgill, the older sister. "Why should we move? This is just like home."

"It is, almost," Mrs. Eliza Pickersgill agreed. "Though I do find the winters hard to bear."

"It's only a question of determination," Mrs. Amanda told her.

"I'm sure you're right," Mrs. Eliza replied. A short time afterwards, Mrs. Amanda had to return to the restaurant by the back door, to keep an eye on the chef, whom she suspected of secret drinking. Mrs. Eliza shook her head. "She'll never admit it," she told the two men, "but the cold puts a strain on her heart. This hill, too. She insists on walking up to the supermarket." In a moment she followed her sister inside the restaurant.

The shoemaker had been thinking of other things. "There's a conspiracy in the air; all these offers at the same time. I think I'll ask a few questions."

For someone who considered himself a socialist, Bartholomew Sacco had many lines of information in the political establishment. He had run for city council a few years before, in a comfortable district where no one was interested in politics, and had won by default. In the brief period he had held office, he had almost lowered property values by his efforts to have a disused school turned into a haven for the unemployed. At the next election, of course, his opponents had got together and, at great expense, mounted a successful campaign against him. But in his time in office he had become friendly with many policemen, taxi drivers, reporters, and others who could search for information. "I'll find out about this," he told Mr. Gottlieb.

Two days later he entered the bookshop. "It's a man named Abercrombie," he told Mr. Gottlieb.

"Ah," the bookseller said, with little surprise. His wife remained silent. Nonesuch, who had been watching from the bookcase nearest the door, grinned with his needle-sharp teeth. The shoemaker explained. "He wants to put up a big hotel here. The plans are all drawn up, and there are even some bids on them. All he needs is the land."

"That's too bad," Mr. Gottlieb said. "It's our land."

"We'd better be careful," Bartholomew Sacco told him.

"Why?"

"He's new to the city, but he has quite a reputation. He came with a lot of money and bought a big house, a regular country estate. He seems to be a whiz at putting together real estate deals, often with more of other people's money than his own. He's also very adept at getting out of deals before they fold, with his own money intact."

"He seemed a well-read man," Mr. Gottlieb remarked. "I wouldn't expect we have anything to fear from him."

"*You* can say that?" his wife put in. "Haven't you known enough well-read men in your own time?" Mr. Gottlieb smiled in a guilty fashion.

"He didn't become rich by being a nice guy," the shoemaker insisted.

"Whatever he is, he can't drive us out of our homes and businesses."

"No. But he might try," the shoemaker said.

In the next few days, all of the owners received further telephone calls from the real estate agents and the lawyer. The prices offered went up, by the same amounts, they noticed. "Did he think we wouldn't talk to each other?" the shoemaker commented.

The Pickersgill sisters received another telephone call that night, though fortunately Mrs. Eliza picked up the receiver. "Don't you find the climate unhealthy?" a young man's voice asked.

"What?"

"It's much more healthy elsewhere. I don't understand how you can stay here."

"Who is this? What do you want?"

"You are living in a very unhealthy location," the voice said. "You really should decide to change it." The caller hung up.

"Who was that?" Mrs. Amanda called.

"A wrong number, dear," her sister replied.

But she could not sleep. Past midnight, two motorcycles roared past the terrace, turned, and passed again and yet again, pausing to gun their motors before the restaurant each time.

Mrs. Eliza told of the call only after the next incident, two days later. Samson was carrying a number of parcels to the post office after school. As he walked along a hidden part of the road, by a high fence, two young men came up on either side, knocked his feet from under him, and scattered the parcels in the gutter. When Samson tried to stop them, they knocked him down again and rubbed his face in the mud. Then they ran off, giggling.

Fortunately the boy was able to rescue most of the books in the parcels before the water could get through the wrappings. He dried them off on his pants and carried them back to the bookshop. He had also been carrying a book he had just bought for himself, an old geology text. As he had told Mr. Gottlieb, "I think it's time I really learned something." This book had fared much worse. It was completely soaked, and a fold-out chart that showed the different ages of the earth, with dinosaurs here and there, was ripped half across. Mrs. Gottlieb spread the chart on the table to dry, where it stayed all day long. "But it's ruined, really," Mr. Gottlieb said. "It suffered in the line of duty. I'll find you another one."

Over Samson's and her father's protest, Rachel took the newly wrapped parcels to the post office to be mailed in the little green Volkswagen, of which she had the use today. When she came out of the post office, she found a tire half deflated and heard the sound of a commotion further down the street. A blond young man in a blue windbreaker was running, his hands over both ears, cursing loudly, though without imagination. "I saw them letting the air out of your tire," the grandmother on the corner, who controlled traffic at this time for the schoolchildren, told Rachel. "I would have stopped them, but I had to watch the corner. Then, when I could look again, I saw that one begin to jump up and down and swat at his ears. There seemed to be some kind of big green insect buzzing round him. I never saw one like it before. At first I thought it might be a bird, but a bird that size surely wouldn't attack people. Anyway, his friend, the bald one, tried to swat it with a piece of lumber and hit blondie on his head instead. I called out, 'Police!' and they both began to run, with the insect, or whatever it was, following them. His friend took off down the alley with the creature buzzing around his head too."

"Who are they?"

"Trouble-makers. They dropped out of school last year; now they hold up little children for their lunch money. They're the ones who roughed up your boy earlier. I was really going to call the police, but maybe I won't have to.''

Nonesuch kept watch along the route to the post office for the next few days. Samson had insisted on carrying the parcels again, in order to be able to pay for more advanced texts on geology. He was not disturbed during this time. However, the dragon was sleeping inside when the next attack came.

Very early one morning, a few days later, several cans of garbage — well-ripened old restaurant refuse — were emptied out before all three buildings. Mrs. Eliza Pickersgill was fortunately out early enough to clear most of it up before her sister saw it. ''I dread to think what it might have done to her heart, coming on it all like that,'' she told Mr. Gottlieb, who was shovelling up his own sidewalk. ''She was furious at the little she saw.''

Professor Ash watched them from the terrace. Shortly, he walked across, beside the shoemaker, who was hosing down his part of the sidewalk and waiting until the bookseller had finished shovelling so that he could wash his sidewalk as well. Professor Ash spoke to the shoemaker, who nodded briefly in agreement.

That evening, all the owners received telephone calls, with still better offers for their property. Mrs. Amanda said drily that she wasn't interested. Mr. Gottlieb said, ''What is all this? Are you threatening us?''

''A threat?'' the agent asked. ''Have you heard a threat? Our firm is the most respected in the city. We don't do business that way.''

''Who wants to buy the property?'' Mr. Gottlieb asked.

''A confidential client.''

''You should watch such clients.''

''I can assure you our client's financial position is sound.''

"I'm sure it is." Mr. Gottlieb hung up.

Bartholomew Sacco simply hung up without any discussion. "Why waste the effort?" he said. He began to make some telephone calls, in Italian.

"He's talking to some of his friends in the longshoremen's union," the parrot told Nonesuch, who was keeping his own watch outdoors and who had perched on the shoemaker's sign. "They owe him favors from the time he fixed their mimeograph machine during the strike, when none of the regular printers would handle their leaflets."

"What will they do for him?" Nonesuch asked.

"Who knows? They unload ships; maybe he wants them to do some loading for him."

Two nights later a pickup truck driven by a blond young man drove by the three buildings. At each, a young man with a shaved, polished head, riding in the back, emptied out the full contents of a very large garbage can. Neither of them noticed Professor Ash, who sat at a table on the terrace, wrapped in an old grey blanket. In the darkness he could easily have been mistaken for a bundle of laundry. The professor, who often had difficulty sleeping at night, had volunteered to keep a lookout instead of reading in his own room. Now he tossed some pebbles at the window above Mr. Sacco's sign. Instantly a light went on and the shoemaker picked up the telephone.

They learned what had happened the next day. The truck had stopped halfway down the hill, just long enough for the unloader to jump down and into the cab. At the bottom of the hill, the pickup found its way almost blocked by an old panel truck that had skidded across the road. As it stopped to negotiate around this obstacle, two large longshoremen opened the doors on either side and pulled the occupants out. They held them silent with hands over their mouths while a third longshoreman very quietly set down two empty garbage cans from the truck. He helped the others load the young men into the cans, which they then pushed down the sloping street. The cans rolled quite a way before crashing over a low curb and into a ditch. Two of the longshoremen drove away in the panel truck, following the third in the pickup. It was driven past the harbor to a soft stretch of beach, where it was parked so that the incoming tide would cover the motor. Someone sent a tow-truck to haul the pickup to the scrap-yard next day.

"We might have a little peace now," the shoemaker remarked.

However, the lawyer who had called the Pickersgill sisters now called them all the following evening with another offer. All refused. "He's not pretending any longer that different buyers are interested," the shoemaker remarked. "I wonder what will happen next."

What happened next was partly due to the physical nature of their hill. One side rose so steeply that at its peak it almost overhung the restaurant. From this point, two nights later, someone tossed a small bomb with a timing device that made it explode at four in the morning. The small greenhouse behind the restaurant was shattered; its side was blown over into Eliza Pickersgill's herb garden. The kitchen window was blown out as well. The cook, who slept beside the kitchen and dreamed of atomic bombs, rose up shouting that one had come at last. Mrs. Amanda ran out with a baseball bat in her hand, cutting her feet on the broken glass. Her sister, talking in a soothing voice, finally persuaded her to come inside.

The police arrived almost immediately, but they were never able to discover the culprit. In another half-hour an ambulance came to the door. Mrs. Amanda had suffered a heart attack, fortunately a mild one, as Mrs. Eliza told her neighbors the next day. "I was so afraid this might happen. She can't stand such excitement," she said. She had to leave immediately for the hospital. Mr. Gottlieb promised to keep an eye on the workmen who were starting to repair the kitchen.

The damage was not so great after all. The restaurant opened again for business two days later, with an unusually large number of customers because of all the excitement. The cook and the waitresses handled them valiantly. Mrs. Eliza had to keep leaving to see her sister in the hospital. When the bookseller and the shoemaker called to her, she answered briefly, averting her eyes.

Three days later they learned from the same lawyer who had called before that Mrs. Eliza had agreed to sell the restaurant. "She's thinking of her sister, of course," the lawyer remarked, very sympathetically. "I understand Mrs. Amanda Pickersgill really needs a less active life. There are wonderful quiet places in Florida, with no hills and no conflict."

"They are joint owners," Mr. Gottlieb pointed out. "Has Mrs. Amanda agreed to sell too?"

"I'm not sure if she has," the lawyer said, "but she will decide to, out of consideration for her sister if not for reasons of prudence and health." He did not repeat his offer for the bookshop, but urged Mr. Gottlieb to contact him if he wanted to sell.

# CHAPTER XIV

# IN A FOREST GROVE

N THE FOLLOWING DAYS, NONESUCH HARDLY LEFT
the bookshop. This was not only on account of his own special treasure, the Book of Hours. From time to time he crawled into the cupboard in Mr. Gottlieb's study to look at it – for the bookseller was too worried to take it out. But mostly, Nonesuch realized, he spent his time watching over the other books in the shop.

Why was he so concerned with these books? They didn't even stay in the shop. They were sold; people took them away, often with eager faces, and sometimes brought others to take their place. It was like the old days in the Abbey of Oddfields, he finally realized, when he had set himself to guard the crops which, he knew, would be harvested and eaten, and replaced with fresh plantings. These books were the crops of the bookshop, Nonesuch thought. Curiously, this idea pleased him. My friends have good crops, he said to himself.

Friends! How he had come to be involved in the ways of humans! Sometimes he wondered if his grandmother would approve. Then, he thought, this must be an aspect of human life that even she had never really known. If we must be involved with humans, he told her in his mind, these are the kind of humans we should choose.

The next message from Mr. Abercrombie was delivered personally. Nonesuch was there to see it arrive. He had found a convenient upper molding that gave him a good view of the shop — and from which he could surprise the occasional black-beetle, for he knew he must keep up his strength these days. From there, he heard the bell on the door announce Huberman, the fat man who had taken away his *Booke of Martyrs*. He stood in his blue suit, his side pockets bulging, drawing pink gumdrops out of one pocket and yellow ones out of the other.

The little dragon left his molding, flew down, hoping Mr. Gottlieb would take his time to enter, and crossed between the free-standing shelves to the one closest to the fat man. As Mr. Gottlieb came into the room, Huberman bumped against the table of paper-backs, knocking a dozen to the floor.

"So many books," he remarked. "They're so crowded you can scarcely pass through."

Mr. Gottlieb picked up the books and looked politely at Huberman's girth. "There's more room on the other side," he observed.

"Oh, but space is definitely a problem here; I can see that. You really need more space. You should expand, even. There's a lovely shop on Brick Street, next to the bank. You could get it for a very good rent; the owner is in trouble, as I happen to know."

"Who are you?"

"Huberman's the name. Already I'm a customer." The fat man held out a sticky hand.

Mr. Gottlieb ignored it. "Are you working for the man who wants to buy my shop?"

"I have that honor," Huberman said fervently. "That man is a genius!" he added. "I'm not worthy to touch the hem of his garment, as the Book says."

"Are you speaking of Mr. Abercrombie?"

"Shh," Huberman warned him, "no names, please." He looked soulfully at Mr. Gottlieb. "You really should sell."

"Thanks for the advice."

"No, honestly." Huberman's voice became very earnest indeed. "You should see the plans for his hotel."

"So it's at the planning stage already."

"And far advanced. It will be a palace! Three towers, the middle one fifteen storeys high, flanked by others of ten storeys. A revolving restaurant at the highest point. A beacon for ships in the harbor! On this very spot will be a glass-fronted promenade, so that the guests can lounge or stroll in all weather and enjoy the view. You should see the plans yourself: you'd be proud!"

"No thanks."

"But really," Huberman said, "I must tell you that construction of such a hotel on such a hill is a major engineering feat. It requires untold skill and imagination. This is why you have all been left alone so long."

"We've been grateful." Then Mr. Gottlieb added, "Fifteen storeys! That will cut the light from the houses above. What does the building code have to say about that?"

Huberman shook his head and swept his left hand back and forth. "This whole section is in process of being rezoned, restructured, reorganized. I won't bother you with the details. What is today a senior citizens' home tomorrow may be a parking lot, and vice versa. This is progress. You wouldn't stand in the way of progress, surely?"

Mr. Gottlieb looked at the harbor and the old houses on the

hill. "This edifice, this monument we are discussing: do you plan to call it the Hotel Abercrombie?"

"There is certainly no thought of that. In fact, my mere suggestion made his lip curl. No, it's sufficient that he *knows* it is his. My employer is a very simple man, basically."

"I'm sure," Mr. Gottlieb said.

Huberman looked very sad and flicked a speck of dust, which might have been a tear, from his eye. "But you are making him unhappy. You should agree to sell. Perhaps the offer was too low; if so, that is a problem that can be overcome. Money heals all griefs, as the old saying has it. Confidentially, what was offered to you is less than it will take to furnish one floor of the hotel. Name your price."

"But I like it here."

"Of course," Huberman told the bookseller sympathetically, "but we all have to give up something."

"I've given up enough already," Mr. Gottlieb told him. "I've moved around enough, too. I'll stay here."

Huberman sighed. "Such obstinacy! You know," he added confidentially, "there will be a small bookshop at the hotel itself." He looked around and shrugged. "Of course, lighter reading than your present stock."

"I imagine."

"I could arrange for you to have that concession. You would still be a bookseller, in practically the same spot; but with no financial worries."

Mr. Gottlieb merely smiled.

Huberman nodded sadly. "That was *my* suggestion. My employer didn't think you'd be interested, but he said I could always ask you. He's reluctant to take more direct action."

"What direct action does he have in mind? More garbage or a better bomb?"

"What are you saying!" Huberman raised his hands, as if in horror, and stepped backwards, crashing against the shelf on which Nonesuch was crouching. His coat pocket pressed back, an inch from the dragon's nose. On an impulse, Nonesuch slipped inside it. It contained lint-covered gumdrops, an old pencil, a rubber band, and a grimy notebook. What was he doing here? the dragon asked himself. The fat man might put his hand in his pocket at any moment. Then he saw a hole in the lining and put his head through it. Daylight shone beneath, where the lining had become detached from the fabric. If he remained quite still, he could travel wherever the fat man went, in the pocket or hidden between the lining and the fabric. The conversation continued over his head, muffled but still clear enough to guide him.

"We admit no knowledge of any such incidents," Huberman told the bookseller. "But, in any case, we'll soon have the restaurant next door."

"If the other owner agrees to sell."

"We have her sister's signature. We have made commitments on that basis, heavy financial commitments. Mrs. Eliza Pickersgill will be responsible if Mrs. Amanda Pickersgill persists in not agreeing. Mrs. Amanda is a very strong-minded lady, a very admirable relic of the old school, but she has a weakness for her sister. She would not want to see her financially ruined."

"Did you think of all that?" Mr. Gottlieb asked. "Or was it your employer?"

"I give him full credit," Huberman said.

"So do I."

Huberman mopped his forehead. "Why do you make me talk this way? Do you think I like it? I'm a kind person, basically. If all those concerned considered their real interests, there would be no conflict.''

Mr. Gottlieb nodded, thinking. ''Well,'' he said at last, ''a warmer climate might be more suitable for both the Mrs. Pickersgills. So perhaps we'll be neighbors.''

Huberman looked surprised. ''Unquiet neighbors, however. We'll tear the restaurant down. The dust and noise will be very disturbing. I was told to mention this. We might rebuild the whole place from the inside, making new foundations, which would generate an incessant pounding. I should imagine your customers like a quiet atmosphere.''

''Yes, and I'll see that they get one!''

''But what can you do?'' Huberman asked, genuinely curious. ''Everything on our part will be done with strict legality. As you will find if you bring the matter to court.'' He had opened his hand and was studying a note in his sweaty palm. ''You have heard of 'the law's delays', but probably have not yet experienced them first-hand.''

Mr. Gottlieb saw him reading. ''Are those your employer's words?''

''He does have a gift for words.'' Huberman returned the note to his pocket. It touched the head of the dragon, who did not stir. Huberman looked round the shop again. ''So many books! I hope you are well insured.''

''Insured!'' Mr. Gottlieb said.

''Against fire. All these dry, inflammable objects might be thought to be a fire hazard. *Can* books be insured against fire? But, even if so, could they be replaced?''

''You'd better go,'' Mr. Gottlieb told him.

''Smoke detectors?'' Huberman asked anxiously. ''Do you have smoke detectors? You should. My apartment is tiny, but I have three of them. You must keep the passage to the outside door clear, too, in case you have to leave suddenly.''

''Get out!''

Huberman sighed again. ''Such hostility! Why do you direct it at me? I'm only a messenger.''

''I got your message,'' Mr. Gottlieb told him.

Huberman looked at the bookseller's white face. ''Yes, I think you did. We hope to have *your* message soon.'' He looked at the table and half drew out a book about luxury automobiles. He glanced at Mr. Gottlieb as if to ask the price, then changed his mind, sighed for the last time, and walked out of the shop.

Both Nonesuch and Mr. Gottlieb had thought they were alone in the shop. However, shortly after Huberman had left, Professor Ash shambled in from a dark corner where he had been quietly sleeping. He watched the bookseller, whose eyes were passing over each volume in turn as if he could thus protect them. ''I didn't see you,'' Mr. Gottlieb told him.

Professor Ash scratched his head and began to search the shelves labelled ''Myths and Legends''. ''Where is it?''

''What?''

''I'm sure I read it,'' Professor Ash said. ''Among the dragon myths. I've been thinking about dragons recently. Those that hold back the waters, and release them; those that hold the earth together but could very easily let it be destroyed. In fact, some of them may want to do this.''

''I know the legends,'' Mr. Gottlieb said.

''But I read another one somewhere.'' Professor Ash's voice was puzzled. ''That some dragons are thinking of destroying the universe but that they refrain because that would make other dragons, who still live among humans, unhappy. Have you heard that one?''

"No, I don't think so," said Mr. Gottlieb, his mind on more important matters.

"I'm sure I've seen it somewhere." Professor Ash continued to search the book shelves.

 Mr. Abercrombie sat on the terrace of his house, overlooking the sea by Butcher's Point, which had taken its name from the slaughterhouse that had been there years ago. Times change, he thought: this would be the theme of the talk he would give to the Chamber of Commerce when his hotel was opened. He would recall the very humble beginnings of his own estate, now located on some of the most valuable property on the coast. New roads, which had permitted one to drive to the city in a quarter of an hour, had brought the value, a sure sign of progress. He made a note in the leather book at his elbow on the glass-topped table.

His speech would depict himself as an agent of change, of progress, a good citizen who had replaced three piddling businesses employing two waitresses and a drunken chef, in addition to the owners themselves, with a modern hotel, the pride of the city. He could picture the faces of the city council members, their eyes shining with greed. He had arranged that each one would profit from the hotel. How they would be edified to think that they, too, were good citizens!

His smile faded as he thought of his last conversation with Huberman. It might have been a mistake to use him at all, though the man was energetic, could follow instructions, and was too stupid to be disloyal. But his manner was gross, it must be admitted; and that dreadful suit, which before had been another sign of the man's inferiority, had now become disgusting. He even picked up insects, it seemed! After he had arrived two weeks ago, to report on the success of his hints about a fire, some large green bug had emerged from a hole in the tail of his coat and flown swiftly into the bushes. Since that time, Mr. Abercrombie had carried out all his business with Huberman by telephone.

In any case, it was better to keep his distance from Huberman from now on, in case the strong-arm stuff brought repercussions. Violence could be useful. It had, in fact, showed the weak side of the two sisters and given him the foothold he needed in the property. Though the others had dug their heels in. He had been surprised to see them offer this much resistance. It was just as well that he himself had visited the bookseller. How surprised the old man must have been to find that another literate man would want to take his little paradise away. And what a joke that Mr. Abercrombie's interest in books had brought him to the shop in the first place and shown him this fine opportunity.

Well, other steps would have to be taken soon. Mr. Abercrombie made a few entries, in code, in his notebook. It was unlikely that either the bookseller or the shoemaker were heavily insured against accidents on their property. Such people usually looked on the bright side of things and trusted to human nature. Huberman had already hinted at reliable people who could take a fall inside a shop, trip over an obstacle — say a crate of bargain books on the sidewalk — or dart in front of an automobile on the way to the post office: all accidents that could lead to ruinous lawsuits. He, Mr. Abercrombie, had also spoken briefly to the inspector from the fire department, who was dissatisfied with his present position and was extremely interested in a post in the new hotel. Both buildings could easily be declared fire hazards, to be set right at greater cost than their owners could afford.

Mr. Abercrombie sighed. To have to step around so, when it really wasn't necessary! Sooner or later these people would have to bow to the inevitable.

Raoul, the gardener, passed by with a wheelbarrow. Mr. Abercrombie called to him. He stopped, bowing respectfully, his face turned aside. Mr. Abercrombie had thought to put mirrors here and there so that he could see the hidden look of hatred on that face. "Have they found the sheep yet?" he asked.

"No, señor," Raoul answered. "Not a sign of them."

"Not a sign? That's too much to believe. Even a rustler would have left some sign. Your friend must have stolen them."

"He is honest, I swear!"

"Of course he is." Mr. Abercrombie smiled and dismissed Raoul with a nod.

But it *was* a mystery, he had to admit to himself. Where had all those animals gone? There was, of course, no chance that Raoul's friend, Henri, the old French herdsman who worked for the gentleman farmer in the next estate, had stolen them. This neighbor had a fine flock of Nova Scotia sheep. A week ago they had started to vanish, that was the only word for it. At first, one, then another; then two, then three, then six in one night. The fences had been triple-checked. The watchdogs would have been on guard, too, but they had vanished as well as the sheep; the first one when two sheep were taken, the next on the following night. There were a few scraps of wool where the sheep had disappeared, but there was hardly any blood. It was almost as if something had flown off with them. And not only from his neighbor's farm. The same thing had been happening in farms all along the coast. First one or two lambs, then an older sheep, then more. The newspapers said that as many as fifty full-grown sheep had disappeared.

Where could they all have gone? Someone must be having a fine feast, the reporter concluded.

And the mystery had not begun with the sheep either. Now Mr. Abercrombie recalled hearing Raoul and Henri talking together in the kitchen before all the troubles began. All the mice had disappeared from the barn; the rats were no longer prowling round the garbage dump. "All God's little creatures have fled," Henri said. "The Devil must be ranging." Both men had crossed themselves, trying clumsily to hide the motion from him.

Mercedes, Raoul's wife, appeared on the terrace and gathered a basketful of logs from the pile by the wall. He had told her to light a fire in the stone fireplace just inside, in the library, against the cool evening. She was a squat Indian woman from Guatemala, who had entered the country illegally, with her husband, a year before. She never smiled. From what Raoul, that excellent gardener, had said, she kept thinking of her sister, whose husband had disappeared and who had refused to travel north with her; Mr. Abercrombie had stored this piece of information away, if only to warn himself that to ask about her family, in ordinary politeness, would evoke a flood of tears.

He had been right to keep his distance, he realized again suddenly. Mercedes came running out on the terrace. "Un dragón en el fuego!" she cried. "Un dragón entre las llamas!"

Mr. Abercrombie looked at her until she controlled herself. "A dragon in the fire?" he asked.

"Yes, señor," she gasped, becoming overwrought again. "A small dragon, in the flames. She is laughing at me!"

Mr. Abercrombie shook his head patiently. "Have you been drinking again?"

"I don't drink, señor." Mr. Abercrombie continued to smile, shaking his head, until Mercedes began to sob and ran from the terrace. He knew that she would control herself soon enough. Perhaps she would even want to apologize for her fit of hysterics, as she had tried to do before for bursting into tears when he had called her in to a dinner party to meet the guests who had enjoyed her excellent cooking. Now, as he had done at that time, Mr. Abercrombie would remain scrupulously polite, as if nothing had happened, as if he could not understand why she was becoming upset again.

Neither she nor her husband could leave him. They knew, for he had told them, that the immigration authorities would investigate them more closely than they could stand, if they tried.

He recalled that his fourth wife had referred to this couple when *she* had left him, to the fact that he kept their salaries so low, even though he himself was relatively indifferent to money. "You could pay them so well that they'd never want to leave you," she had said. "All these manipulations, all the wheeling and dealing, all your activities on the fringe of the law. That horrible goon of yours, Huberman, who tracks mud on my carpet! You're a bright man. You could be completely ethical and still rich. Does it give you any pleasure? You just want to see people dance to your tune!"

He had looked at her with more respect than at any time in the year they had been married. He had almost asked her, "What else is there to do?" If he had given himself away, he would have added that people bored him. They held no more surprises for him. He knew how they were motivated, how they could be forced to act. It was better to be one of those who called the tune, not one who danced.

A trace of wood smoke had passed through the open door.

That was a queer conceit of Mercedes: a dragon in the fire. It must be an old Indian belief; he could ask her about it, but he preferred never to admit being ignorant of anything. The university library would certainly have something about it or even — he grinned — the bookshop. Perhaps when the old man finally gave up, he would sell it books and all.

On the table beside him were two decorating schemes, already submitted to him for the hotel's lobby. One was silver and blue, sea colors. He had almost chosen this one, but now the second, of silvered mirrors, black, and old gold, appealed to him more. The photographs made him think of palaces of Renaissance Italy, of rulers who were absolute tyrants, answerable to no one. He would think about this on his evening walk. A scheme like a Renaissance palace was not ideal for a seaside hotel, he knew, but the view would more than make up for that, and, really, he need please no one but himself.

That period of history must have been on his mind. On the table was also a copy of Machiavelli's *The Prince*. Now he leafed through it to the passage that told how princes should deal with conquered people: ''For it must be noted, that men must either be caressed or else annihilated; they will revenge themselves for small injuries, but cannot do so for great ones; the injury therefore that we do to a man must be such that we need not fear his vengeance.''

He himself hardly need fear vengeance, be the injuries he had done small or great, Mr. Abercrombie thought. In these tame times people were civilized and slow to vengeance — or at least vengeance of the kind the Italian diplomat had meant.

He put *The Prince* on the decorators' files and set off for his evening walk, his head still buzzing with thoughts of times long past. He was in the wrong century, he told himself, one in

which he still had to observe some forms of law and pay some lip service to what was called ''democracy''.

Mr. Abercrombie followed his customary route: down the gate to the main road, along it for a quarter-mile, back into his own property by a hidden path, through a meadow to a small forest of spruce trees. There was a clearing in this forest, around a grove of three old willows that filled up most of the space. From the centre of these willows he could look back at his own house; at Raoul spreading mulch on the rose beds; at Mercedes up on a stepladder polishing the glass door to the terrace, glancing fearfully at the reflection from the fire. In the other direction, he could look across the bay to the harbor, and to the hill above it, which, in one way or another, would soon be his. This was his view every evening: he could look over his property, present and future, without saying a word.

But he did say a few words as the great green shape rustled through the spruce trees and fixed him with its golden eyes. ''A dragon,'' Mr. Abercrombie said. ''Ridiculous!'' The dragon moved closer.

''I don't believe in you,'' Mr. Abercrombie told the dragon. ''You are an illusion. You can't possibly exist. I don't accept you,'' he stated boldly to the gaping mouth, to the fierce, pointed teeth.

# CHAPTER XV

# A BOOK DRAGON

# E

ATING MR. ABERCROMBIE  WAS THE HARDEST ACTION

of Nonesuch's life. Killing him was no problem: his head came off at the first snap, and landed in a bed of chrysanthemums, looking very surprised. If that had been all there was to it, Nonesuch could have taken the proper satisfaction in dealing with his mortal enemy, roared in victory, spread his wings, and flown away. But he knew he couldn't just leave Mr. Abercrombie's two parts lying there. This might give him away or, worse, implicate his friends of the bookshop terrace. No, Mr. Abercrombie had to disappear completely; and in a few minutes he had done so: cashmere sweater, gold Rolex wrist-watch, and all, everything went down the dragon's throat. He made a very large, full meal. Before it was over, Nonesuch, who was still no more than twelve feet long, began to think he should have waited until he was larger still. But he had not dared. Huberman's threat of fire, an attack on both his home and his treasure, had made it imperative that Nonesuch deal with the source of these threats as soon as possible. "Get your tasks done as well as you can, even if not as well as you like." Had his grandmother said that? She might well have done so.

But he learned, as he could have done in no other way, the real reason that dragons in their wisdom had stopped eating people. After he had clawed up the ground to cover Mr. Abercrombie's blood — the police would wonder about these marks, but what could they make of them, after all? — he paused to look around him. How the world had changed! At some distance was Raoul, the gardener, quietly weeding the chrysanthemum beds. Before, Nonesuch had always liked to watch this man at work because of his skill, his love for growing things, and the deep sadness in his eyes. Now he thought, "The ignorant peasant. From the way he looks at me, he doesn't appreciate how well off he is here. He must have forgotten about the death squads. I should remind him."

Nonesuch looked at Mr. Abercrombie's house, built fifty years before by a wealthy man who loved beautiful work. "It's all mine," he thought. "All the carved-walnut shelves in the library, all the planning of the gardens, the ornamental shrubs that took thirty years to come to full beauty: they are mine, I bought them." He looked at the city. A new hunger seized him, full as his stomach was, as if he could never be satisfied. "It is not mine yet," he thought of the city. "I hate everything that is not mine!"

Nonesuch shook his head at this new madness. It cleared sufficiently for him to realize he must hide. He had already picked out an almost deserted island offshore on which he had planned to stay, fasting, until he had regained his old, small size. The rational part of his mind told him he must go there as soon as possible, even though another part suggested that he wait here until people came looking for Mr. Abercrombie and give them a *real* surprise. He waited impatiently for darkness. Automobiles passed on the through highway half a mile away.

The idiots, he thought, going from one place to another, as if it mattered where they went! He was grateful when an evening fog came down, masking his flight out to the island.

The reason dragons should not eat people, he said to himself, as he lay among sumac bushes not far from an empty cottage, was that they took in the people's thoughts along with their flesh. How long would Mr. Abercrombie's thoughts stay with him?

During the following days, Nonesuch rested within sight of a quiet tidal pool full of seaweeds and starfish. He sneered at any fishing boats that passed, but was careful to keep out of sight. At night he set out on long flights, to use up as much energy as possible and reduce his size more quickly. He soared along the coast, just within sight of land, not wanting to approach the world of men any closer. Always he returned to the tidal pool. It was so exposed to any passing boat that at first he had to look at it from a distance. Later, when he had shrunk enough so that the tall grass hid him, he would lie by the pool for hours in the daylight, watching butterflies flit along its surface. Mr. Abercrombie's thoughts had, at last, vanished along with the rest of him.

It took Nonesuch several weeks to reach his old size, but before that, while his wings still spanned a foot, he flew back to the bookshop. He knew it would be more prudent to wait longer, but he was quite unable to keep away. "Well, you've certainly grown," the parrot told him. "If it's still you."

"It is."

"You really do look like a dragon now."

"I always was a dragon," Nonesuch said. "I always will be."

"I never really doubted it," the parrot told him. "My eyesight must have been at fault. Why are you larger now?"

"In fact," said Nonesuch, "for a time I had to be a great deal larger than this; there was something I had to do. I'm growing smaller again."

"By choice?"

"Yes; it's a question of diet."

The parrot shook his head. "Well, whatever suits you," he said politely.

Nonesuch flew out over the parapet to look into the book-shop window, then returned. "I'm eager to get home again," he confessed. "I've been worried about my people. These ones know how to live but sometimes they need help. I have to look after them. And my book too, of course," he added dutifully.

The parrot looked at him with new respect, then cleared his throat. "In your present size," he observed, "you might teach that cat a lesson. He's become very aggressive."

Nonesuch's eyes gleamed. "I'll consider it."

The parrot nodded, then changed the subject. "You certainly missed a lot of excitement around here."

"Tell me about it."

The main events, the parrot said, were visits from the police inquiring about the man who had wanted to buy all the property, Mr. Brian Abercrombie. He had simply disappeared, without apparent reason and leaving no clues. He had gone for a walk one evening and never come back. It was true that the surface of the earth had been disturbed in a small grove of trees on a remote part of his property, but further digging did not turn up a body. Certainly, the police had said, he would have been unlikely to leave of his own accord just when he was on the verge of completing an important business deal.

"My master said to your bookseller afterwards, 'Maybe the Devil himself carried the wretched exploiter away. If so, I'll thank him.' "

Mr. Gottlieb had seemed relieved, but less happy, the parrot said. Perhaps he had been moved by the plight of Huberman, who had been hanging round the terrace like a lost soul ever since his employer had vanished. Huberman had lost his centre. He bothered the police with so many questions and fruitless leads that they told him to keep away from the station. He begged those he had threatened and harassed before for any news, for any suggestions of the cause of Mr. Abercrombie's departure. He kept coming back to the bookstore, which seemed to provide some contact with his departed master. He also took the opportunity to sell back the *Booke of Martyrs* and other historical books, all excellent editions, which Mrs. Gottlieb suspected he had stolen from Mr. Abercrombie. ''From what I hear, he must have had quite a library,'' she remarked. ''I hope we have a chance to bid on it.''

''Why do you think it will be for sale?'' Mr. Gottlieb asked her.

''I just have a feeling. Would that fellow dare sell *any* books if he thought his boss was coming back?''

Huberman apparently did not think Mr. Abercrombie would return, for after two weeks he had gone in search of his lost master. ''I'll seek him throughout the world,'' he had told the shoemaker at this very spot on the street, just in front of the parrot's perch.

''It may be his fate to search a long time,'' the dragon remarked. ''Possibly he'll never stop looking.''

The parrot had still other news, much of which he had learned first-hand. The shoemaker, not feeling it safe to leave him alone, had started to bring the parrot to the restaurant table on the terrace on Friday evenings. When it had become clear to the Pickersgill sisters that no further attempts were being made to take their restaurant from them, Mrs. Amanda began to think more seriously of her health. She and Mrs.

Eliza were now planning an automobile trip to the deserts of New Mexico, which, they understood, combined warmth and dryness with space, a view of mountains, and a sense of history. If they found a place they liked well enough, they would retire there. For the time being, they had asked the Gottliebs' daughter to manage the restaurant in their absence. Rachel, who had found that the bookshop did not keep her busy enough, had accepted gladly. There had already been some talk that if the Pickersgill sisters did decide to retire, they would sell the restaurant to Rachel and her husband. The bookseller and his wife had already told the young couple that they could help them make this purchase.

Nonesuch learned all this in conversation with the parrot over several days. While he was still as large as a pigeon, he stayed on the flat roof of the shoemaker's shop beside a tiny greenhouse full of cucumbers. He watched all the comings and goings from a concealed spot beside a drainpipe. Once, when the white cat, Powder-Puff, who would climb anywhere in pursuit of a bird, disturbed his rest, Nonesuch sent him off screaming across the roof-tops and down to the ground by the restaurant's back shed. Cats in this century didn't show as much fight as they had done five hundred years ago, he reflected: perhaps the earlier felines were more accustomed to the sight of dragons. From then on, Powder-Puff took so many precautions to assure himself that any bird he stalked was not really a dragon that most escaped him.

By eating nothing and by flying vigorously at night and on misty days, Nonesuch soon became small enough to slip through the crack in the wall over the *Distant Voyages* sign and enter the shop again. He is there to this day.

So far, with the help of the humans in the shop, he has kept quite busy enough. Perhaps he has had help from another source, too. When the weather became cold, Mr. Gottlieb decided to reduce his heating bills and installed an efficient wood-stove in the bookshop. The stove's fire shines brightly through its glass front, and it gives out enough heat to warm the upstairs apartment as well; the basement furnace is seldom needed. Professor Ash, who has been finding the cold weather harder to bear, likes to sit by the stove, reading and dozing, sipping occasionally from his bottle and watching fire shapes through the glass. The old man talks more and more with Samson, whose reading has branched out from geology to paleontology and archaeology; now he is back to reading myths, which he once considered too childish. He has become bored with school, always does his homework at the last minute, and as a consequence is only third in his class. One day he spoke to Professor Ash about the belief of some primitive tribes in taboos and evil spirits.

"They see nature that way," Professor Ash told him. "But some spirits are friendly as well. The Irish peasants put out milk for the fairies, the 'Little People'." He laughed. "If I was superstitious, I'd put out something for the spirit that helped us when it seemed we were going to be replaced by a hotel."

"Do you mean the big financier who disappeared?" Samson asked him. "Do you think the Little People carried him away?"

"I wouldn't be surprised."

Samson made a face. "He'll come back yet."

"I *would* be surprised at that. I had a feeling of finality about his departure."

"So, are you putting out a bowl of milk?" Samson asked.

"No, that wouldn't be suitable. In fact," and here the professor laughed, embarrassed, "I don't quite know why, I think the right thing is a book."

"Well, there are plenty of those."

"No, I mean to put a book out. I had that idea, somehow. I left a book open on the table there." Professor Ash pointed to a small desk by the window. "I was interested to learn that the late Mr. Abercrombie, or at least the departed Mr. Abercrombie, had been reading Machiavelli's *The Prince* on his last day with us."

"What's that about?" Samson asked.

"Oh, how people act; how to keep power in the real world. You'd like it."

"I'll put it on my list," Samson said. "But did the Little People read it?"

"The pages were turned, but that might have been the wind."

"Didn't you watch?"

"Oh, you mustn't do that," Professor Ash said anxiously. "The good spirits don't like that, and you might lose the blessing." He yawned. "But I'm becoming forgetful. You'll have to remind me from now on; or you can do it, when I can't."

So, certain books have been left lying out on the little table near the stove, towards the end of the day when it is unlikely that the Gottliebs will replace them on the shelves. Sometimes the pages have been turned, and sometimes not; from the number of pages, Professor Ash and Samson can judge the progress and the literary tastes of the invisible reader – if it is not all an effect of the wind. After *The Prince*, they tried the short stories of Guy de Maupassant (in English translation), some novels of Dickens and Mark Twain, and a history of Rome by Tacitus and of Greece by Thucydides. The invisible reader apparently preferred history to fiction. Special interest was shown in the first part of Macaulay's *History of England*, though eventually even this reader found it heavy going. One day Professor Ash had the idea of taking the *Booke of Martyrs* again from the shelf. In the morning it was found open to the account of the deaths of Bishops Ridley and Latimer. One page was weighted down with a small pebble; on the facing page was a fragment of a gold chain bracelet that must have fallen through a crack in the floor. ''Someone must want to give us a present,'' Professor Ash said.

After other books, other gifts arrived, also presumably from beneath the floorboards: a sapphire that must have fallen out of a brooch and a rare 1914 quarter. Professor Ash looked it up in the coin catalogue and whistled at its current price, but neither he nor Samson has any thought of selling it.

No one else has been let into the secret of this game. Mr. Gottlieb may suspect something, but he has the feeling that when good luck has come, it is foolish to endanger it by too close questioning of any little local mysteries. At times, Samson is sorry that he cannot come back to the shop at night to discover the reader. But he does not even think of discussing the question of its identity with anyone besides Professor Ash. He is especially afraid that if Peter Levy learns what is going on he will lie in wait for the reader, or even set up an infra-red video camera to observe what occurs at night.

During all this time, Nonesuch has kept a good watch on Brother Theophilus's Book of Hours, his treasure. It is as beautiful as ever, and he regards it with deep affection, since it brought him into the present world of books, which, frankly, interests him more now.

But, of course, he has no thought of leaving the Book of Hours. He remembers his grandmother's comments, which once led him to believe that the continued existence of our galaxy might depend on the safeguarding of this book. Now that he lives in the present day, in what might be considered a more rational environment, he does not know if he should really believe his grandmother. Perhaps she was only recounting a grandiose myth, as an old lady dragon might do. But he does not think it wise to take a chance: he has lost enough homes already, and he realizes that conditions that will keep his *Book of Hours* safe will also preserve the bookshop in which it is lodged.

For the same reason — since it may be very important to all of us that Nonesuch not be disturbed — the exact location of the bookshop cannot be revealed, nor its name, though DISTANT VOYAGES is a close approximation. If you wish to know more about this shop, you can pass over the northeast coastline of North America with the wings of your imagination and scan all the islands, bays, and promonotories. If you find a likely spot and look at it very closely indeed, you may see a small dragon perching among the bookshelves.

T H E   E N D